# Seeds from a Silent Tree

## An Anthology By Korean Adoptees

Edited by

*Tonya Bishoff & Jo Rankin*

# Acknowledgments

We extend our deepest appreciation to all of the contributors for their courage to share their voices.

Our thanks to Raymundo Becerra, Miles Hamada, Elaine Kim, Theodore Kim, Jon Owens, SoYun Roe, Marianne Tobin, Eric Wat, and Mitsuye Yamada for their invaluable assistance and advice.

*Dedicated to those who*
*break the silence.*

# Contents

## Reunions

## Seeds of Resolution

*x*

# Introduction

*Seeds from a Silent Tree* emerged from absence searching for presence.

For Korean adoptees, as for many other transracial adoptees, the image of a family tree is twisted, convoluted, severed, splintered, grafted, and for some, withered. Scattered indiscriminately, over 100,000 Korean children have been adopted into the U.S. alone, living in a different country, speaking with different tongues, different names, and different perspectives.

*Seeds from a Silent Tree* explores the embodiment of both and neither. In the spirit of the origin of anthology [from the Greek *anthos*, flower + *legein*, gather], both professional and novice writers gather here to explore the complexities intertwined in transracial adoptions. Through poetry, fiction, and personal narratives, Korean adoptees speak in their own voices, struggling to negotiate an individual space that fluctuates according to their soil, environment, and nourishment—emotional, physical, spiritual.

While there are positive experiences, there are many other life-long struggles to find a place in a portrait without reflection. Some denounce their Korean ancestry in order to survive in their adopted land. Some reunite with their birth families, recovering pieces of themselves. Some struggle with factors infesting families biologically connected or not. Some have set down their own roots by creating their own families. Some did not survive the uprooting and subsequent transplantation.

There is no "right" way. Each individual forms his or her own survival tactics. Despite sharing a specific common origin, we have attempted to present a wide range of perspectives--variations on a deceivingly singular theme. The work is loosely grouped into four sections: *Roots Remembered and Imagined* (images of Korea and birth families from memory and fantasy), *Transplantations* (exploring issues of identity, race, culture, and sexuality), *Reunions* (adoptees meeting their biological families),

1

and *Seeds of Resolution* (individual solutions, both tragic and triumphant). Various pieces overlap, resisting limited classification—just as the identity of Korean adoptees defies rigid categorization.

With this anthology, we seek to break a certain silence—silence from our land of origin, silence from the lands we now inhabit—tongues tied by racism, some external, some painfully internal; tongues tied by social mores, codes, and contradictions; tongues tied by colonialist myths of rescue missions and smooth assimilations.

We hope to shatter these illusions, sowing new seeds for future generations not to be silent—to seek out themselves and each other, to define, re-define, explore, and question. We hope to inspire others, as they have inspired us—to speak honestly, truthfully—and to learn to listen in the same vein.

*Seeds from a Silent Tree* creates presence through creative voices speaking out for their own sanity, paying respect to those who came before, and priming the soil for the survival of those who will follow.


Tonya Bishoff
San Juan Capistrano, California 1997

*Roots Remembered & Imagined*

# Explosions

*(Seoul 1975)*

## Beth Kyong Lo

Mangoes fall from whispering trees
by a police station.  Babies
flood in and out like seashells
rumbling from ocean waves.

Abandoned in Yongsan,
where scrawny sluts swing
in cramped alley corners,
she is wrapped in a bundle
among exploding fruit;
pieces of green shell tear

through army skies.  One
splatters against her head
and grows into a swollen grape
on a withered weeping willow limb--
a motherless, fatherless,
peopleless dust.

# The Living Ghost

## Eun Jung Che

If, at night, the pain was strong enough
He would lie awake and imagine her
Perhaps she would look like him
Or maybe like her mother.
In his mind, she was the ancient
She was the ancestor who shaped his life

He tried to envision her, the unseen,
        by looking through the faces of the past
Creating her, feature by feature, until she was whole
She haunted him even in his waking hours
        The living ghost

And then the ache would become so intense
        that he would go to the mirror
And he would stand there for many moments
Wondering through his agony, "Are the tears flowing from my
        eyes or hers?"
Was it his own image reflected back to him
Or this ghost who is yet undead?

But it was not only at night that his chest throbbed with pain,
He would often think he saw her face, or heard her voice
And yet, how would he know?
He could only search through the chasms of his mind
And like a puzzle with infinite combinations
He contrived her face over and over again
Each time, the face had changed
        the eyes a little smaller
        the mouth a little softer

She would now be nineteen and it was time to create a new
        image
Was he replaced by another man, those around the body
        those arms that should've been his

Did she grow to be beautiful, would this restlessness never end?

Nineteen years this craving has been building
He wished, if only for a day, that he might be granted reprieve
That he might not break his stride and cover his face,
        aching for his daughter
That he could feel fulfillment, that this pain might be swallowed

But then exhaustion would wrap around him and obliterate
        these hopes
And the ache would begin anew

He would climb back in bed, defeated,
        and sing to his lost baby girl a lullaby
Rocking himself to sleep

# New Beginnings

## Sherilyn Cockroft

When I was 4 years old, I remember playing with my older brother, Young Eu, age 6, in a cornfield next to our house; it was in the late afternoon on a summer day. Soon a frantic gentleman came running and yelling that my oldest brother, Young Soo, age 8, had fallen into the river. Immediately, neighbors and friends ran to the river to look for him late into the night, but to no avail. The next day, his body was found on top of the river with foam all around him.

The gentleman was a neighbor of ours, and he and Young Soo had gone fishing earlier that afternoon. When they had finished fishing, the gentleman told my brother that he had mud on him. So my brother went back down the side of the muddy bank to wash himself off. In the process, he slipped on the mud and fell into the swift, dark river. Because I was so young, I was not allowed to go to the funeral, and I never saw his body again.

My father, who lived in another town with another woman, came to the funeral and it was at this time that I remember seeing him for the first time. My first memory of him is that he took me for a walk. We walked hand in hand over the bridge of the river that my brother had drowned in. My next memory of him was about a year later when he came for a visit, and we had a picnic at my brother's grave. I believe that it was a national Memorial Day. Other than those two incidences, I do not remember him visiting our family. However, my father did financially support my mother, brother, and me.

My brother, Young Eu, and I always had a very close relationship. We played together a lot, and being the older brother, he also took care of me and protected me. I remember that we used to enjoy going on many walks together through the countryside. One day on our walk, we found some peach trees. We picked the unripe, green peaches and carried them home in the "pouches" we made with the front of our tee shirts. When Mom saw our "little treasure," she made a very sweet, sugar water and soaked the peaches in a bowl overnight. The sugar water penetrated into the hard, green peaches, and they became sweet--what a treat!

Being the youngest and the daughter, my mom gave me special attention. One afternoon, she brought out a beautiful dress which she had just finished sewing for me. The dress was made of baby blue, sheer fabric with lots of ruffles and lace. In addition, it had so much netting underneath, it stuck straight out! That afternoon, a local photographer happened to come by with a camera on a flat bed cart. Therefore, I put on my new dress and got my picture taken. What a great memory that is--as well as my life with my mom and brother.

When I was 6 years old and my brother was 8, Mom went into labor and a nurse came to our house. Mom delivered a baby girl. For many years, it did not even occur to me that the baby could have been fathered by anyone else than my father. I am not certain, but I suspect that the baby was an illegitimate child. Soon after the baby was born, our mother told my brother and me that we were going on a trip, but she did not tell us where. She packed a lunch of rice and seaweed rolls, hard boiled eggs, and drinks. We got on a train which we rode for quite some time. When we got off, I believe we were in Pusan where Mom's parents lived. I met my grandparents for the first time; our grandfather was especially nice. He was kind and soft spoken. However, our stay there was quite short, only a day or two.

Then our little family continued the trip, first boarding a train, then a boat, and then another train. When we reached our final destination, we had arrived at our father's house. My first sight of him was on a ladder picking persimmons off the tree in the backyard. That night, we stayed with our father and his second wife and child. The next day, our parents got a divorce. My brother was devastated! He cried and cried as our mother boarded the train with our little sister to go back home. I, on the other hand, was quite nonchalant about the whole series of events. Dad tried to console us by buying candy, but my brother was still distressed and cried uncontrollably.

11

Life at our father's house was miserable. Our father was a carpenter and a construction worker. He would be gone for days or weeks working on city roads. While he was gone, our stepmother was quite abusive. She not only verbally abused us, but would withhold food from us as well. It seemed that she did not want her world to change with the raising of two additional children. She had her own child, a daughter, to take care of.

One day, we told our father of her abusive treatment toward us. Upon hearing our stories, Dad became violently angry at our stepmother. The alcohol which he drank that night fueled his anger even more, so he threw a vase at her. This display of outrage tremendously scared both my brother and me. However, when Dad would leave again on business trips, the abuse from my stepmother only intensified. And even with the intensified physical and emotional abuse, we never told our father again.

After several months of living at our father's house, my brother decided that he and I would run away and go back to our mother's house. At this time, I was 7 and my brother was 9. It was a summer afternoon when he took my hand, and we ran across the field behind our house to catch a moving train. The train depot was not far, so at the time we hopped on the train just as it was gaining momentum. We rode the train for almost two hours. When we got off, I believe we had arrived in Seoul. It was about 7 p.m. We had no money so we could not eat. That night, Young Eu and I slept in a stationary coal box car. The next morning, he hopped on a moving bus and tried to help me on it. However, being tired and hungry, I could not move fast enough to board it. And...that was the last time I saw my brother.

As the bus sped off with my brother on it, I stood in the middle of the street bewildered and shocked. And with my brother now gone, I felt alone and confused. I had no idea as to what to do, so I wandered the streets. That night, I slept on a bench in a brightly lit park. Many homeless people were also sleeping in the park. I remember being scared and apprehensive among these strangers; therefore, I could not sleep well. The next day, I hopped on buses. The bus drivers never questioned me; they assumed that I was with the other adults. When they realized that I wasn't, they just let me ride. I rode the buses around well into the night because I felt safer there than in the parks. For many days I wandered the streets and rode the buses; how many days, I do not remember.

One evening, I was aimlessly walking the streets and stopped on a bridge. While looking over the railing, a newspaper boy near me started yelling. Soon a group of people surrounded me, as well as a couple of policemen. The police took me to the police station and asked me a few questions. That night, I slept on a bench in the station. The next day, I was transferred to a Nam Dae Moon City Children's Home. At the home, I was very docile and unresponsive. Several days later, a lady from the Ethel Underwood Children's Home for Girls came and chose me as one of the children to be taken back with her.

When I arrived at the orphanage that night, an older girl by the name of Choi Hyung Sook took me by the hand and helped me clean up. After my bath, a clean outfit was given to me to wear. The next day, I was called into the office. The orphanage personnel asked me questions about my family, how I got lost, etc. They also asked me my birthdate, but I could not remember the date. But I did remember having a special dinner with my mother for my sixth birthday. And I remembered that it was a hot, summer day, so the orphanage gave me a summer birthdate of 6-30-66.

Orphanage life was very confining to me. The entrance to the orphanage had a huge, black iron gate and once we (the orphans) were inside that gate, we were not allowed to leave the grounds. The only time we would leave the grounds was to go to school, church, or a special function, which was very rare.

I enjoyed playing with my friends at the orphanage; however, our entertainment was different. We did not even have dolls to play with, so we had to be creative and keep ourselves occupied. One of the ways the older girls occupied themselves, especially in the winter months, was by knitting and crocheting.

Every fall, each child would receive a disbursement of winter clothes. And among the winter clothes, we would generally be given a couple sweaters. If the girls did not like the style of the sweater they were given, they would unravel it, and knit "new" looking sweaters. I would watch the girls knit for hours. Then one day, I picked up a pair of knitting needles and began knitting. The older girls were impressed with my new knitting skills and asked me to help them knit part of their sweaters. I was happy to oblige and to feel included.

While at the orphanage, I was enrolled in the public school system. I enjoyed school, but I also felt very different because I was an orphan. No one was blatantly mean or cruel, but the students knew who the orphans were and that they were poor. The clothes I wore and the food I brought to school were constant reminders of my status. While other children had the expensive, white rice, I brought brown rice. The teacher would remark on how much more nutritious it was to eat brown rice, but I knew that I had brown rice because it was cheaper, not because of its nutritional value.

In the second grade, I remember that my teacher was trying to be nice and helpful, but I found it quite embarrassing. She told the class that I lived at an orphanage and that if any of the children had extra clothes, to bring them to school for me. Later that week, a bag of clothes had accumulated, and I hauled the clothes home to the orphanage. I wished that I could have new dresses instead of hand-me-downs. So when I would see other little girls with their new dresses arriving to school holding their mommies' hands, I desperately wanted to be like them.

Then one day, I thought my chances of being like one of the little girls in the fancy dresses would be fulfilled. I was told by the orphanage personnel that an American family wanted to adopt me. I was shown pictures of the American family and their house. They had two boys who were older than me and one daughter who was younger than me. It was just like how my family had been--two older brothers and one younger sister. They asked me if I wanted to go to America, and of course, I said "yes". So the preparations began. Every few days, I would be given chewable vitamins to eat, and in addition, I made frequent trips to the hospital for check-ups and immunization shots.

Finally the day came for me to go to America in January of 1976. The night before my flight, I was taken to a home which was to help to-be-adopted children get accustomed to the American way of life. I was fed toast for the first time with butter on it. I was eager to have it because only rich people could have this type of food, and this home even had flushing toilets! My stay there was to be for several days, but due to a scheduling conflict, I stayed only one night. The next day, I was given a new outfit of red pants and sweater, and a new coat! Then they drove me to the airport. I traveled with two other children who were about 7 years old, several babies, adoption personnel, and Grandma Holt of the Holt International Adoption Agency. It was to have been Grandma Holt's last trip back from Korea.

The flight seemed long. We had a layover in Tokyo and San Francisico, and the final destination was Minneapolis, Minnesota. My new family was there to greet me. At first they did not think that I was their daughter because I was so small for a $9^{1/2}$ year old, standing 45 inches tall and weighing 45 pounds. After the adoption personnel insisted that I was their daughter, they looked at the hospital-type bands on my wrist and saw their name. The family hugged me and after saying goodbye to Grandma Holt, I left with my new family. We stayed in a hotel the first night because my family lived in Colorado, but they were in the process of moving to Missouri. The next morning, I had my first breakfast of rice crispies cereal with bananas and milk. I was so eager to have it, until I tasted it! It was so bland! My excitement for the cereal and milk quickly deflated. And to this day, I have not been able to enjoy the taste of milk or many other dairy products.

In March, a matter of weeks after arriving to the United States, our family moved to Missouri. My parents had bought 40 acres with a big, white farm house and a barn. The area where we lived was very rural and the nearest city of 100,000 people was 30 miles away. My parents felt called to the ministry, so they started a small church and a private school.

That fall, my siblings and I attended the new school. The education program which my parents used was one in which each child could accelerate at his/her own level. This program worked well for me because I didn't know any English when I came to America. Therefore, with the curriculum, my father's time and attention, and a great desire to learn English, I began to speak, read, and write the "new" language in a matter of months. However, as quickly as I learned the English language, I lost the Korean language.

The early months of living in America were difficult. I missed my 100 friends from the orphanage with whom I had lived for $2^{1/2}$ years. I knew that coming to America would be good and could afford me the opportunities that I would not have in Korea. Even at the age of 9, I remember thinking, "What will I do when I turn 18 and have to leave the orphanage, especially since I don't have any parents?" That thought was frightening to me. However, one feeling was always with me in Korea and in America. I never felt like I "fit in" after I left my mother's house. And this desire to "fit in" and be "normal" has been something I have been striving towards for many years. I have always had an idea of what normality was--to have parents who were not divorced, to live within a certain range of income, to listen to pop music, to go to football games, to go to college, and finally to get married and give my children a "normal" childhood.

However, I didn't have a "normal" childhood. Not that I had a bad childhood, but I always felt different and inferior. Living in the Midwest did not make things easier; the people there were not used to interacting with anyone who was from another culture. Even going to the mall, people would sometimes stare at me because I looked different. On one occasion in my early teens, I remember an innocent child said to me, "How come your face is so flat?" Even though the child asked an innocent question, I felt very uncomfortable with my appearance. Both I and the child's parents were embarrassed and all I could say was, "I guess God just made me that way." Some adults were just as naive about people from other cultures. Strangers would talk to me loudly and slowly as if I were deaf and dumb. And when I would answer back to them in clear English, they seemed so surprised!

As I reflect on my past, there has been a lot of good which

occurred in my life, as well as a lot of challenges. The challenges have made me a stronger person and strengthened my faith in God. This faith has given me an inner peace, and it is knowing that peace which has sparked an interest in trying to find my brother, Young Eu. Remembering how close our relationship had been and knowing how much he always tried to be strong and take care of me, he must feel great guilt for losing me in the city. I know what it's like to have this type of "false guilt" and for that guilt to weigh a person down. It can be immobilizing. Therefore, I want to release him of this guilt, which he may have, by finding him.

In just a matter of a few days, I will be boarding a plane bound for Korea in search of Young Eu. I have decided to put a hold on my career as an outside sales representative and have accepted a one-year contract to teach English in Korea. It will be difficult to leave everything that is familiar and comfortable, and leaving my friends will be the most difficult of all. However, I know that the time is right for me to revisit my past and to look for Young Eu and let him know that I am doing well, even with the tragic course of events which transpired so many years ago.


*Postscript:*
*Since the writing of this piece, Sherilyn was reunited with her brother and mother in Korea.*

# First Mother

*Kimberly J. Brown*

A mystery
Someone never seen
Existing, but non-existant
Real, but imaginary
The one whose memory is old now
The reflection of the one
Who should have reflected her.
Invisible like the breezes in the air
Transparent, but she does exist
Someone without a name.

# To You Gone at 17 Months

## *Kimberly J. Brown*

The fantasy conversation of a mother to her child

She says,
"I know you look in the mirror
and wonder who it is you see
and
where it is
your mother went.

I can't be there.

But I can tell you this:
I am with you all the time.
I'm in every shadow
your form in the sun
creates

every impulse you experience
once belonged
to me.

I am in the trees
and
the grass
and
the spaces outside
your window.

I am not gone
I promise.
I am with you."

# Biological Mother

## Jo Rankin

You tried your best
To cut the cord
Destroyed a nest
Beyond afford.
My fate was filed
And soon defined
A lonely child
You left behind.
Since you and I
May never be
Together in
Reality,
Should I go on
And try to solve
The questions which
Have since evolved,
Or should I quit
While I'm ahead
And try to do
Without, instead?
Such simple words
For mother's pearl.
From me, with love,
Your Inchon girl.

# The Unforgotten War

*excerpts*

## Thomas Park Clement

*It has been well over forty years since I was last in Korea during the war. It was yesterday.*

### Birth

I lived with my mother as a newborn. I remember my military father coming to take my mother out on the town and leaving me in a cribbed area. I was left inside most of the time because she was unwed and I was half & half....you know....like the cream. Half & half children were a disgrace.

As I lay at home in the dark by myself, there was always the sound of people yelling and crying outside in the busy streets, of mortars and explosions, of sirens to warn the people, when they could, prior to a mortar attack. Sometimes the warning was sufficient. When the sirens went off, all lights at night were turned off so that they would not be easy targets for the enemy to see and hit. I remember standing up and watching the light flashing through the window.

When I was older, old enough to walk behind my father, he would bring me up to the mountains. The mountains were very steep. I would follow behind on a little dirt trail that meandered between poverty-stricken shacks and homes. One time I stopped to stare. Out from a rundown shack, a group of little children came to have a look at me. I was much more fortunate than they. They ranged in size shorter than I to twice my height. They had no shoes or socks, wore rags and were very skinny and dirty. I just stood there and looked at them as they looked at me. I was much more fortunate because I had a mother and father who had clothed me and were taking care of me. I was not thin as bones. My father came back down the path around the corner and asked, "What are you

21

doing?" Curiously smiling at me, he took my hand and led me on our way. He picked me up and swung me around the back of his neck so I rode from this higher view. We could travel much more quickly in this fashion.

The destination was a grandmother, or so I thought, who lived way up in the mountains. There were many relatives who lived there. There was a well with a little roof over it with a hand-cranked pulley connected to a rope and bucket to draw water from far below the depth of the earth. The home was fairly small. It was more peaceful in this mountain home than the busy loud city. I was afforded a lot of attention. My father showed me how to take a stick with a string tied to it and anchor it into the ground. At the free end of the string, he would tie a flying grasshopper to it by the leg. When the grasshopper tried to fly, it would fly around in circles, tethered to the stick. He grabbed my leg and said with a smile, "How would you like me to tie your leg like this and swing you around?" It was a kidding, endearing thing.

*Street Life In Seoul*

As time progressed, the war was coming nearer to its end. There were less and less bombings, less screaming and crying, more hustling about as peacetime approached. There were always air bombing warnings, up until the very day I left Korea.

Life for me, in its more-or-less protected and supervised exis-tence, was about to have a drastic change. One morning, my mother dressed me in a heavy coat and hat. We walked with another lady into the busy streets. We walked for a very long time and I was growing weary. On a street corner, she kneeled down and gave me a hug and kiss. She buttoned my coat as a lov-ing mother would do to ensure the warmth and safety of her beloved child. As she stood up, she instructed me to look down the street and don't turn around. My mother and the other lady walked in the opposite direction. I stood for who knows how long, looking down the road which was filling with people going about their business. When I finally turned around, I was alone.

22

I slowly began to walk. There were many people in the streets now. I walked and walked and walked.....alone.

I ended up in an area that was not very crowded. It was not an alley. It was not a nice area. From behind and from my sides, a group of street kids came running up, surrounded me and, in no time, stole my coat, shoes, socks and hat. They pushed me down and were gone as fast as they had appeared. This made me cry. I began to walk. Another group of street kids approached me. The smaller ones ridiculed me and started pushing and hitting me. One of the older boys in this group stopped them and he stuck up for me. He had more authority over this small gang of kids. The rest of the kids changed their attitude toward me....they could easily see that I was cream. I was not as fortunate as they. They looked all Korean. They adopted me.

We lived on the streets for who knows how long. They taught me how to beg, borrow and steal. They taught me how a small group of little individuals could work as an organized team to overpower grownups to get what was needed to survive the harsh street life of Korea in a time of war and post-war.

Bandits are the name of the wrap-around the military used to secure cargo when they were shipped overseas. We would bend the half-inch wide strips of metal back and forth until they finally snapped free. With this smaller portion, perhaps no longer than 4 to 6 inches in length, they taught me how to sharpen one end into a knife point by scraping it against a stone, building or concrete until it transformed into a sharp dagger. We would then find string or paper to wrap around the handle and spit on it until the handle felt very comfortable to hold. It was important to have more than one weapon because in a street fight, you could become separated from your knife and you had to have another readily available. By making little slits in our pants, we could wear the knives on us unnoticed. We used them for self-protection.

Life on the streets was very harsh. We were a small group of miniature survivalists. We ate anything we could find. I contracted worms. We would beg anyone we could for anything they would give us. Most of the time our requests were ignored.

People would try to get away from us as quickly as possible. One time a soldier gave one of the older kids a piece of gum. The boy split it up into many pieces to share with the rest of our gang. He then tore the wrapper in many pieces so that we could put it into our mouths with the gum so as to increase the bulk of our little piece of gum. It somewhat reminds me of the story of Jesus when he split the loaf of bread amongst the crowd of many to feed everyone.

As the group functioned, a method developed to our madness. We would find an alley which was actually the back side of a restaurant. Many times we could find discarded food here and there. But the food was always cold. One day we were looking down an alley when a shutter of some sort at the back of a restaurant was lowered. It had a rope connected to it on both sides so that the shutter became a kind of table. The store employee, perhaps the restaurant owner, placed a large bowl of hot food on the surface for a very old man to eat. The food was both liquid and solid. The older boys who were stronger and could run faster picked up stones and anything they could throw and started yelling and tormenting the poor guy. They showered him with stones but the old guy kept eating and eating until finally he got up and chased the taunting boys. When he was far enough away from the food, two others ran up to the food and stole the whole bowl. It is very difficult to run with a bowl half filled with hot liquid.

They were smiling and running at the same time, with liquid spilling everywhere. One of the boys in mid-run scooped up some food with his free hand and stuffed it into his mouth. I was the smallest in our group and was still learning how to "get with the program". I did not run away. The old man grabbed me by my arm and started yelling and shaking me violently. He lifted me part-way off the ground and shook so hard that I couldn't see straight. Some of the bigger kids ran up and began to hit and kick him until he let go. Two of the kids got on each side of me and ran with me as we made our getaway. In a place of safety, we ate in silence until the food was gone. After that we laid around watching the retelling of the great heist. One of the storytellers was mimicking how I looked as the old man was shaking me. We laughed and laughed until tears came down our faces. My arm and shoulder hurt for a long time.

Our gang had run-ins with other gangs. The members of our gang were much younger than some of the other gangs. I had a more difficult time on the streets because I looked very American. Actually, I was the only one in our group who looked different. One unfortunate day, or perhaps it was a very fortunate day, another group of street kids surrounded me. They hit and knocked me to the ground. As they held me down, one put a flammable liquid onto my arm and another boy lit it. They moved back to watch me burn. I stood up and folded my arm. Perhaps it was an instinctual thing to put out the flames. I was in excruciating pain. I opened my arm and the liquid and fire had spread to the other side of my arm. The group of kids ran because some people came to my rescue. They took a cloth and wrapped it around my arm which was on fire and smothered the flames. They picked me up and comforted me, dressed the wound, fed me. They asked me many questions which I could not answer. I did not know how old I was, my date of birth, where I lived or where any living relatives were. Later I was on the streets again, my arm wrapped.

It was not long thereafter when a female missionary found me on the street. She kneeled down, looked into my face and asked me more questions I could not answer. She took my hand and we walked. She brought me to an orphanage where I was brought to the director. After asking me many questions, they opened a closet door. In the floor of the closet, there was a huge pile of socks. I ran and jumped into it. I had found the "mother lode"! Both women laughed and told me that I could take one pair of socks for my bare feet. Just one pair. I was very grateful. It had been a long time since I had socks on my feet.

*Life in the orphanage.*

Life in the orphanage was not all peaches and cream. It was certainly, in many respects, a great improvement over the hardships of living wild on the streets. There was a roof over my head.

There were consistent meal times, food, water and clothing. There was supervision. Of course, as in any institution, there are good people and there are bad people. I had my fair run-in with both. I am not going to dwell on the negative, nor am I going to completely omit all of it due to a social message which needs to be brought out to the forefront.

The very first night I was in the orphanage, I could not sleep. Many children were terrified. When the lights went out, they screamed and cried. To get everyone to stop crying, older kids and counselors walked up and down on top of the rows of kids, walking on their legs until everyone would be quiet. A little boy, who was laying next to me with a grin on his face, lifted his covers to show me that by tucking your legs up tightly under your body until your knees touched your chest, one could avoid getting their legs walked upon. If we were quiet and not crying, the older counselor boys walking up and down on children's legs would look down on us and not hurt us. They would walk past. I learned many new ways to survive this new situation.

At night, someone would always steal my covers. It was very cold and I would awaken in the morning shivering. A friend showed me how to tuck all the edges up underneath so my body weight anchored the blankets down and no one could steal them. We looked like little mummies, but we would not shiver from the cold of stolen blankets.

That morning, before anyone else awoke, I dressed myself and tried to get out the front door. It was locked. I was trapped. A counselor awoke, came up to me and asked me what I was doing. I told them that I was going fishing. I was certain that this was not the place for me and I wanted out! She laughed and told me I wasn't going anywhere.

It was very difficult living in the orphanage due to a multitude of reasons. There was not enough money to take care of so many children. There was not enough clothing, shoes, (they must have just received a donation of socks from the States), or supervision. It was very difficult for me to change lifestyles from being wild and free on the streets, although filled with danger and tribulations, to a semi-controlled poorly-funded lifestyle in the orphanage. We were taught songs and were organized to stand in long lines, sometimes two by two, sometimes single file. In the building next to where we slept and ate, we would walk to kindergarten singing songs. There were wooden toy trucks and blocks to play with and in the playground, there was a little manual merry-go-round. It was fun. There was not a lot of food, but there was enough to eat on a regular basis. I did not have to fight for my life against a group of starving street-children, but I had to fight one-on-one against individuals who were prejudiced because I was not 100% Korean. I was a bastard, a disgrace to Korean society.

To go to the bathroom, instead of going anywhere we chose, we went downstairs to a room where there were paint cans. We went in the paint cans. Downstairs was a very spooky place. At night when it was all dark, it was where the bad kids had to stay as punishment. There were always cries of horror from the dungeon. I had to spend a few nights there, too.

*The Adoption Process*

I guess I could tell you about other horrors which happened in the orphanage, but I will not. There is no progressive purpose of wallowing in the negative. I will leave it to your imagination.

The United States passed through Congress an act which allowed the passage of foreign adoptees from Korea. The first group of adoptees was airlifted to the safety of the U.S. and then the act expired. June and Richard Clement, two American citizens with very big hearts, heard about the plight of the many war orphans left behind in Korea. They began the process to adopt a Korean/American orphan. They had to wait until another act was passed. When it passed, they threw themselves at the trials and tribulations involved in being one of the very early international adoptee parents. They put in their requests, filled out many forms, communicated back and forth. We were what is now being referred to as First Generation Korean/American Adoptees. Korea had never exported children out of the country before this time.

When the orphanage realized that I was one of the choices that the Clement family was focusing their attention on through a series of transcontinental communications and exchanges of photographs, my treatment, although I was half-and-half, changed drastically overnight. I became Adoptee Case #500. No more abuse. I was given medical attention. They shaved my head to tend to the infection from the wound I had received from having my head slammed into the floor. In a report to the Clements, they said that I had a ringworm which had to be surgically removed, thus the reason to shave my head. There were no other shaved heads in the orphanage. I was fed more, even got pudgy! I got to sit on someone's lap and try my first sip of coffee. People played with me and almost treated me as an equal.

After the Clements made their final decision and picked me!!!, there was a delay because June was pregnant with a new girl, my future little sister-to-be, Leslie. After she had a successful delivery, the adoption process was on.

The very last day when my escort arrived, I was dressed in new (donated) clothes for my long journey across the waters to the Americas. Someone took me aside, kneeling in front of me, face to face and confided, "Don't you ever tell anyone about anything that happened here or we will come over there and bring you back."

I went with my escort to the airport for the journey. Another little waif who was also being adopted by an American family by the name of Canada was also to make the journey. In the plane I could not sit still. I ran up and down the aisles. Everyone was full of smiles and no one tried to hurt me.

My new brother, Richard, and my new older sister, Carolyn, were brought into the room, one at a time, to be introduced. They both sat across from me and began to whisper to each other and giggle. It seemed that everyone was talking in a strange language. It sounded like Chinese. No one told me, or rather I did not comprehend that there was a language change between countries, so I thought I had grown very stupid overnight. I could no longer understand anyone and no one could understand me. The

Korean language was now obsolete. I wanted to go home.

Everything was different. Lights controlled by wall switches. I would stand up on a chair and flip them on and off screaming, "Fire!" When my mother came home with groceries, it was "Christmas"!!! Why, these new people had Christmas every day! What a weird place.

*Chinks, Gooks and "what have you"*

Throughout my childhood, I was subject to the insensitive ridicule from both other children and grown-ups. I would be minding my own business after a trumpet lesson in town waiting for my mother to pick me up at a street corner where we usually met. Two boys a little older than me came up and shoved me to the ground and kicked me over and over saying, "Hey Chink, where'd you get those funny eyes. Ha ha ha! You little twerp."

My mother would arrive later knowing that I had gotten myself into some kind of scuffle. When she asked me what had happened, I could only sob. I never could say, "Some prejudiced little boys beat me up and called me a Chink." Perhaps she knew without me saying. There was nothing I could do at the time. There was only me living in a predominantly white society with a few black people living on the other side of the tracks. All that I could hope for was that someday I would grow up big and strong and be able to take care of myself....and five or six others!

What is it in people that they feel so afraid of others who look different than themselves? People who they have not a clue about? What if my name was Bruce Lee? During my youth, the world did not know about Bruce Lee. What Bruce did for the Asian community was to have all people in the world think that every Asian person could kick your ass. Thanks Bruce.

*Red*

It was in junior high that I had a run in with "Red". He was a good

5 inches taller than me and looked very strong. I, on the other hand, was slight, almost skinny. I was standing with three girls and a boy, feeling okay about myself. Hanging around with girls was a new thing. Red came up to us with a couple friends. He pressed his hands to each side of his temples and pulled back which made his eyes look a little more like mine. He stuck his front teeth out and gurgled some sounds like he was trying to sound Oriental. He called me a "Chink" and left laughing with his friends. That night I began to practice in front of the bathroom mirror. The door was locked. I looked at my eyes and opened them as wide as I could stand without them hurting. I used my fingers. I looked at them closely in the mirror where my nose was almost touching the mirror. Yes, Red was right. They did not look like his. He looked like he saw a ghost all the time. I looked like I was smiling all the time. I needed to see more ghosts.

# November

## *Zoli Seuk Kim Hall*

one day they arrived
wrapped in white blankets
as tight as larvae

they slept snug inside the cradle of the nurse's arms
and then were lowered into the cribs
like fat grains of rice

i watched one pucker her steamed bun face
as i stood above her metal box,
the black wisp of her hair

pulsed above the vein,
like a small bird breathing across the fontanel
of her sleep.

she was my first child then
i could turn my life towards her
and not look away, as the faces of our own lives

had done to both of us.
now waiting there in that moment together
inside the vacant womb of the orphanage

littered with abandoned tinker toys
and children's faces across from me like passing trains
moving through the tunnel of that day

we were temporary passengers of each other,
which one of us would be left tomorrow?
what became of voice, ear, lock of hair?

i stopped looking for the sisters of familiarity,
in front of me during the daily prayers,
the back of each girl's head i used to memorize

reading their own length and root
like the pattern of a vase
one would disappear one morning

and vanish into the shape of the world outside
the thumbprint of their companionship
aborted from the room of us

the hour of finding one of us gone would move on
the shift of fingers reaching for the half globe of the rice bowl
the bird chirp of the bomo's order to "eat"

the task of the day, to fill it with the rhythm of the living,
a clock's hands ticking towards the night
the missing piece of grief

a silence slowly lowering in my throat
the sharp edges of that wordless word
poking through the chattering commotion

of the nurses gathering into the corner
dividing the air with the edges of their talk.
the clip boards pressing against their chest

when the watches on their wrist would clock the hour of depar-
ture
the chosen infants then lifted like prized dolls
and held up to the door of the house

i watched the backs of the nurses, their white coats
like ships sailing into the mouth of the exit
and above their shoulders,

the ringing static of a baby beginning its cry
and the chorus vibration of the other infants joining in,
into the history of the world taking them back into life

the door shutting between us
i wondered if they knew then
who would be left behind to remember them.

# If I Could Go Back In Time

## Sam Rogers (Kim Sun Il)

If I could go back in time I would like to change what happened when I was six and a half years old. I say that because I saw my real father die. It is not a very pretty sight to see a loved one die right in front of you. It all started one morning in Inch'on, South Korea. My father had two jobs, one as a carpenter and the other as a truck driver. He took me to some neighborhood I had never seen before. He and his workers were just putting the finishing touches to a house they were building. He took a ladder and climbed up onto the roof to check the shingles. Just as he took his last step onto the edge of the roof, he slipped and fell. As he was falling, I rushed towards him trying to catch him but I didn't get there in time. I said, "Father, Father, are you all right?" And all he would say to me was, "Take care of the family."

One of his friends took us to our house. The only people at home were my two sisters and my grandmother. My mom was in Seoul working in a coffee shop where she would come home every Friday and return to Seoul on Sunday.

My father's friend helped him get to his bed. My grandmother made food and gave it to my father, but he took it and threw it at the wall. I didn't want my sisters to see my grandmother and father arguing so I took them outside and told them what had happened. My sisters rushed to the house of our neighbor who was a lot wealthier than us and also had a phone. They called my mother and told her to come home. After my sisters finished talking on the phone, I took them back home. When we arrived, I saw my grandmother crying in her chair. I asked her, "What happened?" and she said, "He does not care any more about life and does not want to eat or drink."

Later that day, my mother came home from Seoul. She tried to talk to my father and all he would say to her was, "Go away."

On his very last day, he told me again to take care of the family. Those were the very last words he said to me. My father did not eat or drink for fifteen days. I will never forget that.

I didn't cry right then. I was just shocked. I stayed there for a while and finally told my mom, grandmother, and two little sisters that he had died. That day and night had to be the worst of my life because my grandmother, mom, and little sisters cried all night long. But for some reason, I still didn't cry.

The very next day, we had a funeral. I was up in the mountains where my relatives were buried. I closed the latch of the coffin when we got to the burial site and my friends and family helped me put it where I had to bury him. I remember how a lot of people were crying, the eulogist took a long time and it was all very boring.

When that was over, everyone had to leave except me because it is a Korean tradition for the eldest son to stay back. On the ground I put a red sheet with four big rocks, one at each corner. I put all sorts of stuff like wine, beer, and cigarettes because he liked to smoke and drink. And lots of food. As I was putting the finishing touches, I started to cry. I guess I cried because all of this reminded me of him or maybe it was time for me to cry. I don't really know.

After the funeral, life was much different because I had a lot of responsibility. I was the man of the house. In Korea, the eldest son is in charge and owns everything the father had owned. It was just different because my grandmother was getting old and my mom was never home because she was working all the time. So finally, my mom and grandmother took me and my sisters to an orphanage in Inch'on. It was a very sad moment.

While we were in the orphanage, our grandmother died. Then we got adopted by American parents. From that day on, we never saw our mom again. I have not been back to my homeland.

# For Ugly Babies

## Amy Kashiwabara

"What an ugly baby,"
    her father cooed.
"Yes, the very ugliest,"
    her mother replied.
"And look into those eyes,
    obviously she is very stupid too."
"Yes, very stupid."
    They said this so that the goblins
    would not be jealous and steal their baby.

    When she had a baby of her own,
    she could not be wise.
"You are the most beautiful baby,"
    she whispered when no one could hear.
"The most beautiful baby
    with the most beautiful eyes and
you will always be happy."
    She was silent, helpless, when the baby
    was taken from her and sent overseas.

    Her daughter grew up an American,
    a writer with poems for children.
    She can be mother and father
    and they will always be hers.
"You're very ugly,"
    she says to one.  To another,
"Very beautiful."

# Him, Her, I

### Zoli Seuk Kim Hall

i stand at the front door of a missing memory
with no forwarding address,
my birthmark born from their bodies,
my mind born from their vanishing,

i see my mother's brown black head eclipsing inside the glim-
mer
of his pale moon eye
and the silk bright sleeve of his shirt
floating to the floor.

i am waiting to take shape among
the sum of his legs walking up next to the sum
of her legs, lowering below his belly
his arms pulling her against himself.
i want to walk up to them
and tell them to stop!
turn towards his face and ask "do you know what you are
doing?"
turn towards her face and ask "is he the right man?"
but their bodies keep moving without me, they move against
each other
like the algebra of sex combining into
the equation of resemblance
separating into the cells of my orphan amnesia.

the exiles of their familiar, lives like a constellation
of a thousand molecules inside of me
where he leaves me himself, as the body of a woman, where she
leaves me as the child of her life
looking back inside the broken brown eye of the past

as if it has always been like this
the self of the present watching
her find pieces of her selves, inside the puzzle
of that mirror, gleaming back into her life.

# Unnamed Blood

## *Tonya Bishoff*

i was squeezed through the opening
of a powerful steel bird
that carried me far away,
and with each mile,
i felt the needle
tear the thread
through the moist flesh
of my lip,
and with each mile,
the thread pulled
tauter and tauter
till i could no longer call
for Omoni
i could barely moan--
and eventually
i became silent,
and the silence spread
throughout my blood
and seeped
into my bones
as the bird thrust me
into soft, white fleshy arms
and the afterbirth
poured through my eyes
surrounding me in a
pool of salty
death

and i am thinking
there is more than
a singular
birth place time date
i am hoping so

but dear god,
give me a sign
when the labor pains
will begin again...

*Transplantations*

# *recycled*

*Lee Herrick*

Images melt like succulence
from a Dali vine,
dangling in perfect sun.

My memories were never yellow
but they hint at it now,
glossed from the wind
of too few living moments,

like unpicked ripe food
unpacked from atmosphere,
wrinkled on ant infested hay,
where they drip, drip...drip.

A worm inches to the base of the tree
unaware of the past,
false memories and other irrelevancies,
and begins to digest, blissfully.

# Bulgogi

## Ellwyn Kauffman

*Korean barbecued beef. This recipe calls for a half-pound of rib steak. I have a three-pound tri-tip roast in the freezer. I'll just use that. I'll need ungodly amounts of garlic and ginger and soy sauce. Wine, too. I've got a bottle of marsala. Marsala should work right? I'll just use that.*

Whenever someone new asks me how I got my name, I'm faced with a choice - do I tell this person about my adoption or not? If I'm feeling at ease I usually dive right in. I tell them how in 1973 my sister and I were left in Seoul's Sajik Park on the 4th of July. It was 10:30 in the morning when we were found crying hand-in-hand by an elderly man who happened to be there for a walk. We stayed at Holt Adoption Agency's Seoul orphanage until March 6th, 1974. That's the day when we arrived at the Northwest Orient terminal in the Seattle airport to meet our new parents.

Often I would rather not tell this story. Like paths that lead one to another, this story leads people to ask deeper questions. And sometimes it doesn't seem right, divulging such intensely personal history. Sometimes I tell people I'm adopted and stop talking, hoping they'll get a clue that the questions should end. But there are times when I meet people with no tact or sensitivity. It's when these people insist on delving into my life, like it's some amusement ride, that I resort to the following story. It goes like this--

"My great-grandfather lived in a rural farming area in Korea near Il San, (I have no idea where Il San is, other than somewhere in South Korea). He was still a young man at the time a group of German missionaries set up a small trading outpost near his village. So, you know, of course some social mixing occurred between the Germans and Koreans. Anyway, one night all the men in the village were drinking with the Germans, telling tall tales, eating kimchee and sauerkraut, you get the picture. Now great-grandfather was a good-sized guy, even by German standards. And you know how things get when a bunch of men get together and drink--they've got to prove themselves. The biggest German guy wobbled to his feet and challenged my great-grandfather to a wrestling match. There was no way great-grandfather would have ever backed down from a challenge to his manhood. The stakes were decided like this--the loser of the match would have to take the winner's name for the rest of his life. So a ring was drawn in the dirt and my great-grandfather and the German went at each other like two angry bears, kicking up clouds of dust, and knocking each other all over the ring. The rest of the men pitched in with drunken cheers as the match went on and on and neither man could gain the advantage. But finally, my great-grandfather made a mistake and was pinned. He was angry and humiliated, but he knew it had been a fair fight. Being a man of his word, he took the German's name--Kauffman. And that is how my great-grandfather came to be called 'Kauffman Si Ha'. To this day, there are still a number of Korean Kauffmans living in and around Il San."

Sometimes the person knows I'm completely messing with their head. But most of them buy into the story completely. I imagine these nosy people feeling culturally empowered with this anecdote about a clan of Koreans with German names, rushing off to tell their friends. I've actually heard it related back to me embellished with the sorts of details that only come through telling and retelling. So what if it's something of a defense mechanism? It's great fun. The Korean word for such behavior is "napieyo!" - "bad!"

*I've sliced up an entire head of garlic and the ginger root. Was I sup - posed to peel the ginger first? Too late, it's already in. The sauce pan is brimming with soy sauce, marsala, sugar, and a bit of water. Oh, and I almost forgot, the recipe calls for half a medium apple, quartered and sliced. In it goes.*

In my hometown there was a Korean-owned market where Mom used to stop sometimes to buy milk. I was probably no more than six or seven when I walked in and saw the Korean grocer and his wife behind the counter. The sight of them stopped me in my tracks for a moment. They spoke to us quickly in Korean. My sister and I stood there dumbfounded and embarrassed. Mom answered apologetically, "I'm afraid they don't speak any Korean." The grocer and his wife looked confused and a bit sad while Mom explained to them that we had long forgotten the language. I followed Mom around the store, keeping a wary eye on the grocer and his wife, actually afraid of these people, as if they would snatch me away back to Korea, never to return.

When Mom paid for the milk, the grocer reached over the counter and offered my sister and I each a bag of peanut M&M's. I didn't want them, but Mom made sure I did and said, "Thank you." As we left the market my ears and face burned as the grocer and his wife smiled, waved and said a Korean good-bye. The next time we went in they gave us popsicles. It wasn't long before my sister and I chose to stay in the car whenever we went to the Korean market.

I was ashamed of my ethnicity. All my friends were white. My parents were white. Who was this Korean in the mirror? The mirror was the inescapable reminder of where I had come from. Most days I was able to forget it. But there were times when my Koreanness stood up like a big, barefaced lie I could not cover. I learned to play the mute, and let the hot shame ebb and wash away in its own time.

*The smell of soy sauce is intense. I imagine the steam from the bubbling pot condensing and dripping from the ceiling. The skin is separating from the slices of ginger and floating to the surface. I should have peeled it. I can't imagine any effect half an apple might have on this. It's like tossing a hand grenade into a nuclear explosion.*

*A bookshelf*
*towering above*
*me*
*filled with toys.*

*A mat*

*spread on the floor beneath*
*me*
*I lay down to sleep*
*with other children*
*I see my sister*
*across the room*
*laughing with another girl.*

*In the street*
*soldiers*
*dressed in black*
*arms swinging in*
*steady rhythm.*

*I eat*
*a bowl of rice*
*flecked with small rings*
*of sausage*

*I stare*
*into the sun*
*until I see*
*its white disc pulsing.*

*My Korea.*


*The Hell-broth is cooling now. The house smells like it's been hosed with*
*soy sauce. I taste it before putting it away in the fridge overnight. Ye*
*Gods! Is it supposed to be this salty? My roommate walks by and com -*
*ments that the smell covers up the cat's litter box odor really well.*
*Tomorrow I will toast sesame seeds and slice some green onion.*


The adoption case progress report from Holt states that my sister,
"Kim Jin Young, K-2371... Enjoys good rapport with people at the
orphanage, being obedient to her *bomo* and playing happily with
other children, takes personal concern about her younger brother,
Kim Si Ha, K-2369, always wishes to be with him either at the
table or at bedtime." And later in the report, "Should be placed

with her brother.  According to the child, her mother died and father disappeared."

When we were learning English, my sister used to talk about Korea.  She told of how our birth father had taken us to the park and given us lots of candy.  He told us to wait there, and never came back.  She talked about picking vegetables, and remembered an aunt who disciplined her by making her sit on a hot stove.  There were even vague mentions of another younger sibling.  But today my sister remembers nothing about Korea.  And my own memories only go back as far as the orphanage.

Sometimes I wonder if halfway around the world there is a Korean man who is an older version of me, my birth father.  Does he ever think about me and my sister, about what became of us?  Does he feel regret or sadness?  Is there any feeling at all?  I wonder what must have been going through his mind as he left us.  Was he overcome with sorrow over the death of our birth mother?  Were there other circumstances that I can only begin to guess at?  Did he feel guilty leaving us?  Did he feel he had a choice?

*I don't have a "Pulkoki grill."  So I fire up my little Smoky Joe barbecue. Once the coals are ready I throw a couple pieces of Hell-broth soaked meat onto the grill, where they sizzle and hiss.  The marinade drips and sends flames licking up.  It smells wonderful.  I turn the meat and watch as it curls and falls right through the grill into the coals.*

There is a picture of my sister that was taken when we lived in Washington.  Dad snapped it right as she was stepping off the school bus.  She is wearing a white dress, brown shoes and has a note pinned to her neck ruffle that has her name written on it. She's just let go of the door handle and one foot is still in midair. A paper in her right hand is motion blurred against the black and bright yellow school bus.  The ends of her hair just touch her shoulders, bangs level-straight over her eyes.  And she's wearing the most surprised, natural smile on her face, her head cocked slightly to one side.

But this picture breaks my heart. My sister and I have not been close for a long time. Somewhere between growing up and leaving home we stopped talking to each other, really talking. Every night after clearing the dinner table we would stand side by side and talk about anything that was on our minds while we did the dishes. I miss the free and easy talks my sister and I used to share.

I don't know her anymore. Sometimes I wonder what her personal life is like, whether she has been dating someone, what she does for fun. I don't know anything about her really. I wish she'd stop dying her hair. And I wish she'd take better care of her herself. I wish she could be the happy, outgoing sister that's easy to be close to.

But I can't expect my sister to be the girl bounding off the school bus with the surprised smile, the world to conquer. What does my wanting have to do with anything other than me? I don't know her. I just know what I expect. I ask myself now - am I ready to know my sister all over again, with no expectations? Am I enough of a brother to let her be who she will?

*I nibble from a jar of "Cosmos" brand Kimchee as the rice finishes and I stir-fry some onion and green pepper. I turn the meat underneath the roaring flame of the oven broiler. Almost done now. Three pounds of marinated tri-tip really doesn't look like that much when it's cut into such tiny pieces.*

There were times growing up when I didn't want to be a part of my own family. I would sit at the dinner table and tune out whatever Mom and Dad were saying, and wonder what my life might be like had I been adopted by different parents. Once I remember Mom talking how lucky she and Dad had been in getting us, because there were a few couples ahead of them in line to adopt. In some brilliant fantasy, I saw all these couples standing in a row while I looked them over, picking from their number who I would adopt as my parents.

Perhaps with different parents my family would have been more

49

like the Keatons, the Waltons, or even the Cosbys. We were the Kauffmans though. We didn't have a lawn, we had a cornfield. There were chickens and rabbits in our back yard and we rode around in a '59 Rambler with tailfins. Sometimes people would stare at us, and sometimes do worse than stare. I hated being different and attracting even well-meaning attention. My sister and I must have seemed at times unhappy and unreachable children.

But what a brave thing my parents did, to reach out across race and culture to take us in. To my parents we were children, that is all. They saw no color and held no judgment about our past or where we were from. We had suffered tragedy early in our lives and needed a home and love. And this, along with all its disasters and joys, is what they offered us.

*I scoop rice and vegetables on my plate. Then with chopsticks I take a piece of my first Korean culinary venture, and I chew. Tender. But way too salty, like eating a bouillon cube. I reach for water. I eat more bulgo - gi. I drink more water. I have made soft beef jerky. But the rice is done to perfection. And I am pleased.*

# A Picture in an Album

## Bill Drucker

*Date: 1977*

I was attending Brooklyn College at the time. It was my second go around at college, much to my parents' relief. They felt I could do better than work on an assembly line. On long weekends, I would take a bus from the New York City Port Authority on 42nd and 8th Avenue and travel up to New Jersey. They still had the lakefront home then. It was a rambling ranch style house, heavily shaded by aggressive maples on all four sides. The stifling summers were cooled by the shading of the branches, but there was hell to pay in the late fall when all the leaves fell to the ground. It seemed there weren't enough bags or rakes to get all the leaves. The property gently sloped down to the brick walled lake front. The living room faced the lake and took in a lot of light from the windows on three sides. It was quite pleasant during the summers.

The usual topics of conversation took place between Mom and me. How was college? How did I like city living? Have I found a girlfriend yet?

"Oh, I've met a couple girls. Very modern, very ambitious. They are very busy with getting into law school or applying to medical school. This is the time of the feminist consciousness raising. Marriage is something on the back burner. There are too many other things taking a front seat. Even guys have to stand in line now."

"So, there's no one worth bringing up to the lake?"

"Ah Mom, they're all city girls. They wouldn't know what to do with grass under their feet. Don't worry. The right girl will come along. And you'll like her."

"Just as long as she makes you happy."

I shrugged.

"It's inevitable. Anyway, it isn't the wife you're waiting for. It's the children. Dark hair and almond eyes. I'd have to pry them away from you with a crowbar. You just wait and see."

She pulled out a plastic bag from the drawer in the china hutch. She held it up for me to look at but didn't say a word. It took a while before I realized what it was. The cotton pullover shirt was white with a light blue collar and border. The shorts were light blue with elastic waist. The outfit was cleaned and folded.

I held that bag. "Are these the clothes that I wore when I arrived in this country?"

"Yes," she said softly.

"My God, look at it. It wouldn't fit a healthy three-year-old today. And I wore this in 1960, just a few days before my seventh birthday. You are something else. You kept it all these years."

She took it and carefully placed it back in the drawer.

"Saving it for my kids, are you?"

She just smiled.

That was the last time I saw her. I never did find that outfit after she died.

* * *

Date: 1960.

Brooklyn, formally the fourth largest city in New York, was one of the most bustling boroughs in the city. Brooklyn was made up of sections called Bensonhurst, Canarsie, the Flatlands, Borough Park, Bay Ridge, Flatbush, Park Slope, and toward the ocean to

Sheepshead Bay, Brighton Beach, and Coney Island. The past hailed such landmarks as Ebbits Field, home of the Brooklyn Dodgers, Coney Island, the Brooklyn Navy Yard, and the Brooklyn Bridge. Actors George Raft and Mae West came from Brooklyn. Jackie Gleason came from Brooklyn. Barbra Streisand and Neil Diamond were Brooklynites.

The Brooklyn I knew was 48th Street and Eighth Avenue, a part of Bay Ridge. I attended Saint Agatha's Parochial School. Mom would take my brother Robert and me to Sunset Park on weekends while Dad studied for an engineering degree. We moved to Jersey in the mid-sixties, since the new company Dad worked for decided to move their operations there. If we stayed in Brooklyn, I would likely have attended New Utrecht High. New Utrecht High was used as a location in an early Frank Sinatra and Jimmy Durante MGM musical. If I had passed the entrance exams, I might have attended Brooklyn Tech, a prestigious magnet school in its day.

John F. Kennedy was the national figure of the day. Pope John the 23rd headed the Roman Catholic church. Mass was said in Latin. Superman and Batman comic books sold for a dime. The candy store back then had stools and a counter, a soda fountain, and a griddle. A wall with magazines carried the popular Life magazine. The city papers were printed and sold in morning and evening editions. Outside the store stood a penny bazooka bubble gum machine and a penny jawbreaker machine. The Drucker fabric and cloth store was right in the middle of the block. Above the stores, occupied the front and back apartments. No building on the block stood higher than two stories.

The Mathews and the Druckers lived within blocks of each other. They knew of each other. This was typical of city life. It was also typical to live almost on top of each other and never know it. That was also city life. There was a famous pair of Brooklyn cops in the sixties, high profile supercops, dubbed Batman and Robin. When they got assigned as a team, they found out that they lived within twelve blocks of each other.

My paternal grandmother, Fanny, and my Uncle Sol operated the fabric store as partners. It was quite vogue back then to buy yard goods and to sew your own clothes. The best designers lent their names to dress patterns. Sol was the uncle who introduced me to the joys of Jewish eating. Sometimes, when he made buying trips into lower Manhattan, he would invite me along for the ride. This was the time in the business when the natural fibers as wool, cotton, and silk fought for shelf space with the new fibers, nylon, and orlon. He would give a customer a two-minute lecture on identifying the synthetic fibers.

"If you put a match to nylon, it melts. See, it doesn't burn," he explained with a cigarette in his mouth. He was a chain smoker. "Has the smell of celery."

My parents, George and Joan, rented the front apartment above the store. Dad did not get into the family business. Instead, he worked for Bunge International, an import-export company. Because he could speak Spanish fluently, he managed the cargo traffic from South America. Later, he joined an engineering firm. Mom stayed home to care for their son, Robert. Most of her family were just two blocks up, her mother and father, brother Frank, and older sister Dorothy.

Joan was fair, with light brown hair and blue eyes. She was the youngest of four in an Irish family. Growing up in an Irish family that housed three generations, she learned mostly to clean, being the youngest. Her grandmother ran the house and did the cooking. Her mother shopped and cared for the children. The children did chores and ran errands. When they got older, they got jobs. Frank drove a city bus for the New York Mass Transit.

The first time Joan did any cooking was when she got married. She had gained local notoriety early in the marriage when she set the kitchen stove on fire. The firemen came, and all the neighborhood stood out in the streets. Some hot oil caught on the curtains while she was frying. For weeks afterward, people stopped her on the street and gave her recipes. She got to be a good cook. I recall some good pot roasts.

Like all married couples, Joan and George tried to start a family.

It seemed to take longer than usual just to have their first child. The family doctor eased their minds and offered them some good advice.

"There's nothing wrong. Just relax. Maybe she could stay at home and not work for a while. Get yourselves a dog."

So, they got a dog from the local animal shelter. Ginger, a gentle, short-hair hound was adopted into the Drucker household. Robert came along a year later. The Mathews were ecstatic for George and Joan. Fanny gave her daughter-in-law a peck on the cheek, in a rare show of affection.

Perhaps her large family upbringing and the fact that her sister Dorothy already had six children, Joan wanted more children. It was in this frame of mind, that one evening she saw a commercial on television. The Angel Guardian Home, a Catholic adoption agency in Brooklyn was sponsoring the adoption of Korean orphans. Joan saw a whole different face of war. The countless war orphans. It was only 6 years since the end of the Korean War. Most Americans still carried fresh memories of World War II. Joan's brother Frank had served in Panama. Sol had served in a medical unit in England. George had served in the Army. Most male friends they knew had served in the military.

A turning of the dial, a random commercial, the faces of children from half way around the world. It touched Joan. But adoption. What a thought. It was impossible. Yet, the thought persisted in her mind.

George was simply amazed at his wife.

"Why not another one of our own. Let's wait. There's time."

But the idea of adoption did not go away. Finally she contacted the Angel Guardian Home. It took almost three years to have Robert. We could have another child in a few months, she thought. Maybe a little Korean girl.

In the office of the Angel Guardian Home, they filled out forms, answered a hundred questions. They looked at photo albums, hundreds of pictures of boys and girls. The nun gave Joan the first album, pictures of boys, despite the fact that she had told the sister she was only interested in little girls. The sister apologized and went to get other albums. While they waited, Joan opened the album sitting in her lap.

Joan flipped through the pages, looking at all the faces of little boys. She saw one face and said that was the one. It was me. She planned for a little girl, but she wanted me. What could she possibly have seen in one worn black-and-white photo, a picture probably outdated by at least a year. What did she see that could make her decide and not bother with the albums of orphan girls? What could have touched her heart so completely?

Joan had made up her mind. Once George agreed, she notified the Angel Guardian home. They filled out more papers. They faced state and federal investigation. The Arch Diocese of Brooklyn was involved in the proceedings. Money for fees and services were paid. American names were discussed. She wanted Thomas. He wanted William. The families, amazed at the whole idea, came to lend support. If anyone disapproved, they kept it to themselves. Everybody was too fond of Joan to say otherwise. Marcie, Sol's wife, taught kindergarten and first grade in the local public school. William would attend there.

What should have taken a few months, stretched almost to a year. It pushed Joan to the limits of her patience. First, because Joan and George were of different faiths, they had to promise that the child would be raised Catholic. There was no real contention there. George hardly ever practiced his Jewish faith. Joan was a devout Catholic. Next, the child would attend a Catholic school, and not the local public school. They argued that. Marcie was there to lend full support in defense of the public school. The parochial school would be a definite burden financially. Still, Joan and George agreed. What next? Could they afford another ticket for a Korean student? No, this was too much. The Angel Guardian Home had dragged this to the point of extortion. The agency also held back some information. As far as my adoptive parents knew, they were getting a reasonably healthy child. The first year, they discovered I had polio, mild dysentery. At school, I tested positive for the mantoux tuberculin test.

The adoption process seemed endless. The child could have been dead by now. Joan and George had danced through every hoop. They had agreed to every request. Where was the child? Just when Joan was ready to give up, George asked her one question.

"Do you want the kid or not?"

It was as simple as that.

They came to pick me up at the Idylwild airport, Kennedy International now. I spoke no English. I had traveled half way around the world. I had no idea where I was or who these people were. They drove me back to Brooklyn, fed me, gave me clean clothes, and my first toy, a metal car. They introduced me to my brother. At almost two, Robert stood a head taller. I was just a few days short of my seventh birthday.

I sat at the kitchen table for my first meal in America. Joan ladled chicken soup and rice in a bowl. There was a plate with slices of white bread. She watched as I looked for approval before I ate. She urged me on. I bowed my head, said grace in Korean and methodically ate every drop of soup and last crumb of bread. It went on this way, serving after serving. Her approval before I ate, grace in Korean, wiping the bowl and plate clean. Now, I'm told that I ate all the soup and a whole loaf of bread. I remember the size of that stock pot. It could hold 4 quarts. That's as much as I weighed at the time.

In the following days and weeks, my new family members came to visit me. Dorothy's kids became my brothers and sisters. Marcie taught me my first word in English. She pointed to the toy I was given.

"Car," she said.

We were by the window in the apartment. I looked outside and saw the real cars parked out on the block. I looked at the toy.

"Car," I said.

Fanny lived in the back apartment above the store. I was changing my clothes when she came in for a visit. She was not given to much emotion, but Fanny cried at the sight of my malnourished little body. She was aloof with her own children and in-laws, but Fanny was quite generous with all of her grandchildren, Joel and Myra from Sol and Marcie, Robert and William from George and Joan.

My new mother had one mission that summer. She was going to fill in the first six years of my life with more food and love than humanly possible. When I woke up from a nightmare, she was there. I couldn't speak English very well to explain, but a warm hug soothed away most of my fears. I watched television and learned English. She introduced her two sons proudly to the neighbors.

I heard Dad complaining one time. We had run out of toilet paper. I tore off a piece of the New York Daily News, rolled it into a ball and moved it between the palms of my hands until the paper fibers got soft enough to use. I'm not sure that he used it, but he was quite amused. He told me that story years later.

That fall, in a blue blazer and plaid slacks, I walked to school with my mom. When I saw the nuns, I thought I was being sent back to the orphanage. I begged my mother not to let me go. She held me and assured me nothing would happen. I was home.

\* \* \*

My legal adoption didn't take place for another six months. The adoption system had a window where the process could be dissolved, even when the child was here. A return policy. Change of heart, unfit parents, whatever the reason, I could be sent back.

Joan had set a family precedent. Some years later, her older sister Eleanor adopted a girl and a boy. They were American children. A cousin, Eileen Callahan, and her husband adopted two girls and a boy, all from the same mother. Eileen also went through a Catholic adoption agency.

"As a nurse, would you consider adopting a disabled child?" they asked.

"Yes, I would consider that."

"Would you consider a black child?"

"Sister, my husband and I have no problems with a child of another race or color. But some family members would object, and my mother would never speak to me again."

Her adopted children came from a white American.

* * *

Joan kept in touch with the Angel Guardian over the years. Maybe she still had some thoughts of a little girl. She had learned some distressing news. Around the age of 15, the orphans were let go. Boys could manage to find work as farm hands and laborers. But the young girls, with no skills, often fell prey. Some ended up as prostitutes. Efforts were made to teach the girls sewing and cooking skills. Later, some secretarial skills were added.

Strange thing about adoption. If the process worked 100%, the orphanages would be out of business. But orphanages still exist, almost thrive. In Asia, in Europe, in Africa, and right here in the United States. If she could, Joan would have shut down every one of them.

* * *

*Tuesday, February 17, 1976.*
*Joan Helen Mathews Drucker, wife and mother, died of injuries from a car crash. She leaves behind her husband, George Drucker, and two sons, William and Robert. Services will be held at the Picci Funeral Home, Main Street, Stanhope, New Jersey. Mass will be held at Saint Michael's Catholic Church in Netcong, NJ. She was 45.*

# Behind My Eyes

## Melissa Lin Hanson

### I. Birth

The walls of an orphanage
            my mother's womb.
Concrete slabs quiver and quake
            spit me into the world.
Legal papers and airplane tickets
            preparation for my birth.
Two white people decide to adopt
            that's where life began.

### II. Heredity

Jenny brags
"I have my mommy's nose."
            My hand flies up--
            gentle pats
            yield
            no answers.
all alone  all alone  all alone
No history of my own.

### III. Korea

My heritage is a black hole
so kindly filled in by others.
Sighted
with 20/20 vision
in their ignorance.
            Oh. Koreans. They eat dogs.
            They live in huts and pee on the floor.
            Why are you dating a chink?

Damn refugees!  Go back where you belong.
This is what I knew of my yellow colored skin.


IV.  *Family*

At the Super Valu I skip along.
Dancing
the cart past rows of Lucky Charms.
       Eyes stare.
       Lipstick lines move
       "Is she yours?"
My mother must explain that yes, she adopted me.
Hurtful interruptions.
Accusations.
Inform and teach me that I
am different.
My family is not normal, not natural, not true.
I don't have a real mom and dad
if I am not
their race.


V.  *School*

Oh goody!  Recess!
Amidst whirlwinds of sand and slides, and childhood chatter,
a spinning world--
STOPS.
       Small fingers
       yank
       at the corners
       of his eyes.
       Ugly
       little slits
       in his face.
       Like mine.
Panic electrifies my veins.
Paralyzed by shame
my face flames

scarlet
with heat.
> Head
> snaps back
> in malicious laughter.
> Please no.
> Oh, God.
> The other kids
> saw.

my eyes.  my eyes.
Monster Mongoloid eyes.
They betray me.


VI. *Teenage*

Wonderful indecision
Maybelline berry blush and bubblegum pink lipstick.
Carefully curl the hair.
Lay out Guess jeans for tomorrow.
Yet in the kettle of my gut
bubbles a stenchy brew
> pity, anger, hatred
> tears of self-contempt.

I know I am not pretty.
T.V., movies, and commercials scream so every day.
Even my Seventeen magazines take their side.
> All American beach babes
> shake out
> streamers
> of soft golden hair.
> Breasts displayed
> as if on a platter.
> Long, sexy Nair legs
> prance in a row.
> Luscious lashes flirt
> over big, blue eyes.

This is what I knew of beauty.

*VII. Adulthood*

I have a family.
It is the people who raised me.
I'm studying Korean and I even like kimchi.
Unlearning the lies
      about Korea
      and women
      and the color of my skin.
I can identify what happened to me.
I now have a voice and I can speak my mind.
I can speak and I can write.
I can love and I can fight.
But something is missing.
      My past is lost
      and questions pervade.
      I have a family here, but
      who am I?
I won't be complete
until I come full circle.

# A Few Words From Another Left-Handed Adopted Korean Lesbian

## Mi Ok Song Bruining, M.S.W.

*The Year of The Rat.*

In a few days from today, I will be celebrating my thirty-sixth birthday. As I look back on my life experiences, I realize with some regret how much I have not experienced, yet am learning to appreciate what I have accomplished in my short, long life. I will attempt to share my experiences in this essay.

I was born sometime in September, but my exact birthdate is unknown. I celebrate the date that was filled in on my birth certificate. However, I do not know the exact day I was born. I suspect that I was born on October 7th, of the Lunar Calendar, but here in the U.S., the Solar Calendar is observed, so I celebrate my birthday on September 25th. I was born in the Year of the Rat--this one being my third to celebrate has brought me significant changes & life-altering events.

*Adoption.*

I arrived when I was five years old in 1966 & had lived in an orphanage in Korea from the time I was an infant. I was told that I was abandoned, rejected, & unwanted. My parents told me I should feel grateful & lucky to be adopted & should not feel sad about anything. My adoptive parents sponsored me from the time I was six months old until they decided to adopt me when I was five. I was told by my adoptive parents that they adopted me because the adoption agency told them that I would be a prostitute if I remained in Korea.

My adoptive parents believed that they rescued me--a poor, little, helpless "orphan" child. Perhaps they did, but the psychological damage done to me as a child has been tremendous & has taken years for me to resolve. It is only recently that I have been able to forgive them for not allowing me to grieve & mourn my birth mother, to feel & express sadness for the losses I have experienced. It has taken years for me to realize that their good intentions were hurtful to me, that they did the best they could & that they tried the only way they knew how. It has taken me years to stop blaming, stop resenting them for depriving me of my feelings & for their empathic failures.

My adoptive parents live in Rhode Island & moved there from New Jersey in 1975, when I entered high school. I was fifteen years old & dreaded riding the big, yellow school bus over twenty-five miles away, to a high school three towns over from where my parents lived. Our town was too small to accommodate a high school. I single-handedly integrated this small, provincial, conservative, Yankee New England village by being the only Asian resident. I was most certainly the only Korean adopted person of any age.

When I describe my childhood to my friends, it sounds idyllic & it was in many ways. I had loving adoptive parents and three (non-adopted) siblings, owned a horse, competed in horse shows, had private art lessons, a beach to play on in the summer, two large, involved extended families--cousins, aunts & uncles who were always around, friends, activities & an abundance of everything a child needs to be nurtured & thrive on. Yet, something was very wrong & something was always missing. Being the only adopted person & the only Korean member of my families--immediate & extended--I experienced a great deal of emotional alienation & cultural isolation. I was taught to forget my memories of Korea.


*Horses.*

During my first Year of the Rat--1972, I was twelve & my adoptive parents bought me a horse. That horse was to become my best friend, comrade, confidante, & companion for eleven years. We competed in horse shows together, went to horse camp, foxhunting, trail riding & were actively involved in 4-H & pony clubs. I loved my horse & when he died in 1984--my second Year of the Rat--I was devastated. He continues to appear in my dreams at night when I am sleeping. Often, I am riding him on the beach, which was our favorite activity together. When I wake up, I am overwhelmed by sadness.

*Adolescence.*

My parents didn't know what to do with me when I asked & begged them to take me for counseling when I was fourteen. They refused to take me to counseling. I felt I was going crazy. I read *Sybil, I Never Promised You A Rose Garden* & other books about adolescent girls who were institutionalized for mental illnesses. I believed that I would end up in some institution for the mentally ill. I was convinced I was going insane because I felt so inauthentic. I did not feel white, as I had been raised. I did not feel Asian, as I clearly looked & was.

I could not find a way, did not know how to integrate my false self--in acting & being white like my white, adoptive parents & their three children & my true self--in feeling Asian/Korean--into one complete, whole self. I was both & neither. I was suicidal. I never attempted, but my suicidal ideations were very real. I wanted to die many times and often, from the age of seven & many years after that, I wished I would never wake up when I went to sleep at night. I remember waking up the following mornings resentful that I was still alive. I realize now, that I did not really want to die, I just wanted to end the pain of the loneliness, isolation & alienation I felt for so many years.

Adolescence is traumatic enough without being targeted for being racially different, culturally identified as "alien" & looking like no one else--peer, child or adult. I was stared at, harassed, bullied, called names, insulted, threatened, & verbally abused by other kids--younger & older--on a daily basis--on the school bus, in school, stores, restaurants, & many other public places in Rhode Island. I remained silent, seethed with rage, & internalized tremendous fury, venomous hatred & poisonous disdain.

The only ways I coped were to disappear into my drawings & escape alone on my horse for long, solitary trail rides. I had friends at high school, I was active in drama club & art club & I socialized with my peers who all felt different for some reason, but none of my friends even considered me as an Asian person. I had not made any conscious attempts to identify myself as a Korean individual. I did not know how. I had no role models, no encouragement from my adoptive family, no peers who were Asian & none who were adopted.

I decided not to pursue a career as a commercial artist as my parents had encouraged me, & dropped out of art school in 1983. I felt a tremendous sense of failure & reluctance to pursue art. It took me years to return to drawing & now, I continue to do art work for myself & occasionally for others. I accepted the fact that I was not competitive enough, nor willing to sacrifice my convictions, sensibilities & integrity to become a commercial artist.

*Korea.*

In June, 1984, I returned to Korea as a participant in the Holt Adoption Agency-sponsored "Motherland Tour" with other Korean adoptees for two weeks & toured the country. It was a painful, but healing journey for me to discover my "roots", to remember some repressed memories, to return to the orphanage where I spent the first five years of my life, to eat authentic Korean cuisine for the first time as an adult, & to try to speak the minimal Korean I had learned. This was my first step to reclaiming my identity as a Korean-American woman. It was a painful, profound, but very necessary step for me.

*Boston.*

When I moved to Boston one month after my return to Korea, I joined Asian-American organizations, learned about oppression, marginalization, empowerment, feminism, & progressive politics. I learned to deconstruct all that was taught & conditioned into me about racism, homophobia, sexism, classism, economics, privilege & colonialism. I embraced these new & exciting ideologies, theories, practices & actions into my ways of being, living, life. It was an amazing time for me--a year filled with rage, discovery, empowerment, affirmation, consciousness raising, liberation, sisterhood & socio-political awareness. For me, there was no turning back.

It was in Boston, at the age of twenty-four that I first met Asian-American peers--strong Asian-American women who identified themselves as Asian-American. I did not realize until I was an adult that for twenty-four years, I had felt invisible as a Korean person, I had repressed my cultural identity, & was ashamed for being, looking & wanting to be different. For years, I had avoided looking into mirrors & cultivated my self-hatred, internalized racism, hid my low self-esteem by over-compensating & excelling in art & horseback riding for almost twenty years.

*Speaking Engagements.*

That year in 1984, I started speaking out about the issues of international adoption. First, I was invited to speak at adoption agencies, then at adoption conferences, then at other conferences. Initially, I spoke about my personal experiences & eventually, in what I consider a natural progression of my own understanding & awareness, I introduced the socio-economic, political & cultural issues of international adoptions. Since 1984, I have done over 70 speaking engagements. I have been invited to speak & have traveled to New Zealand, Hawai'i, most of the Northeast & some of the mid-west. I have also had a few articles on international adoption issues published.

*The International Adoption Industry.*

In 1985, I accepted a job at the largest international adoption agency in New England & worked there for a year as a document processor. I was able to return to Korea twice that year & went as an escort to bring adopted children to their adoptive families in the Boston area. It was a painful learning experience working at this adoption agency, but I do not regret one moment. At this agency, I observed & witnessed disturbing practices of racism, hypocrisy, corruption, cover-ups, the destruction of birth information of Korean infants, poor screening processes of pre-adoptive parents & inadequate pre-adoption preparation for pre-adoptive parents.

I suspect that many other adoption agencies practice these tactics in order to export as many children from developing countries as possible. Everything I learned at this adoption agency, I will be writing about in my forthcoming book. My reputation as a "radical & militant" activist for the "international adoption reform movement" is known within the industry. I am considered an enemy to international adoption agencies, adoption social workers, some adoptive parents, & even some adult Korean adoptees who disagree with my known opinions, because I speak my truth & am an "out" lesbian.


*Lesbianism.*

I fell in love with women & came out as a lesbian in 1987. I informed my family & friends. My family observes the "Clinton Policy of Homosexuality: Don't Hold Hands, Don't Tell & Don't Ask". My friends have been very supportive & accepting of my sexual identity. I continue to sometimes skip & sometimes stumble on the rocky road of relationships. I continue to jump off the cliff, take risks & get my heart broken. Yet, I learn from every goodbye--painful as it is, and I don't have any regrets.

In fact, I have met several adopted lesbians in my travels, even adopted Korean lesbians. It is so exciting & reaffirming for me to know that there are other women who share my story, where we can identify with each other & understand each other without explanation. I have also been informed that there are a few lesbian meeting places & two lesbian organizations in Korea!

*Poetry.*

In 1989, I started writing poetry in a serious way. In 1990, I had my first poem published. Since then, eighteen of my poems have been published.

In 1994, I obtained a literary agent in Manhattan. I started writing my book at that time & continue to work on it. When people ask me what I am writing about, I reply that I am writing about international adoption issues. I am writing creative, non-fiction prose written in the genre of memoirs--my story, my experiences, my opinions, my feelings, my life--as a "Left-Handed, Adopted, Korean, Lesbian, Poet, Writer, Social Worker, Activist Who Eats Meat & Doesn't Give a Damn". I also hope to include my poems & illustrations in my book.

*Cambridge.*

This being 1996--my third Year of the Rat, in January, I anticipated unforeseen, life-altering events. I was not disappointed. As I write this, I have returned to Cambridge, Massachusetts for several reasons.

I had lived here in Cambridge & the Boston area for six years, from 1984 to 1990. I moved to New York City in January 1990, then entered social work school six months later. I earned my masters degree in social work in 1992 & practiced social work for three years in New York City. I moved back to Cambridge, to focus on my writing, be closer to my Boston friends, whom I had maintained contact with while I lived in New York City & most importantly, work on a relationship with a woman who lives in Cambridge. We now live about three miles away from each other.

*1996.*

As I write this today, I am sitting here at my desk in my apartment, with my cat, Fiona Feline, sitting by my side. I think about the past--my journey to this destination--one that I am continuing towards & do not know where or when it will end. I am preparing for the future & learning to appreciate the lessons of my past.

*A Gift from the Universe.*

In late June--about four months ago, I received a phone call from Korea. This woman named M.H. heard about me through my friend C.A., who is also Korean, adopted, & a lesbian. C.A. is currently living in Korea for several months. C.A. & M.H. became friends & M.H. is the vice president of a Korean adoptees organization called The Euro-Korean League (E.K.L.). M.H. & E.K.L. held a press conference in Seoul & as a result of the media coverage, Korean Airlines offered to provide a free roundtrip airline ticket from the U.S. M.H. called to offer this ticket to me. I accepted immediately & scheduled my trip to Korea for December 1, 1996.

I plan to stay in Korea for one year--to learn Korean, teach English (for income), search for my birth mother, travel, write & do research for my book. I am very flattered, excited, & thrilled to have been given this opportunity. I consider this opportunity a gift from the universe, at a time when I did not know whether I wanted to remain in Cambridge. The day before I received the phone call from M.H. in Korea, the woman I was involved with decided to break up our relationship.

*More Losses & New Hopes.*

I was heartbroken by the loss of this relationship & now, I realize that it is time for me to go, it is meant to be, the universe, the Goddess, kharma--something is telling me that I need to go--to find myself, learn more about myself, my birth country, my Korean heritage, my cultural identity, my mother tongue. I am hoping that I will write in Korea. I am hoping that what I write will be the final chapters of my book. I have been dreaming of returning to Korea since 1985. I am eagerly anticipating my experiences in Korea as a journey of discovery, growth, fulfillment, struggle, healing, & learning.

71

*Autumn 1996.*

I have friends who are Asian, African-American, Latina, mixed-heritage, white, & Jewish. I have friends who are lesbian, gay, bisexual, straight, married, single, adopted, non-adopted, older, younger, radical, fierce, "mainstream", women, & men. My white friends are interested in, supportive, & accepting of my Asian identity. My Asian friends do not think I act "white" & in fact, feel I am very Korean-identified. I am very comfortable with my identities as a Korean lesbian, as a Korean adopted woman & I struggle with the economic limitations I have chosen by focusing my life as a writer, poet, artist & activist—working & living in the margins, outside the limitations of "mainstream" society.

I am paying the consequences of my decision to not continue working in the social work profession, yet I believe that my dreams, my goals, my passions, & my vision will guide me to where I want to go & who I will become in my life. As I prepare to celebrate my birthday, I realize that my life gets more difficult, continues to be a struggle, but improves & gets better & better each year. I am humbled, grateful & appreciative of that. For me, it's all about process & progress.

# China*

## Kari Smalkoski

*A given place becomes our temporary home, and yet we preserve a suffi - cient distance to feel its strangeness, not perceived by those who live there permanently.*
    *-Czeslaw Milosz*

I have adopted Korean radar, I'm sure of it. Perhaps all adopted Koreans have it built inside. We come battery equipped once we're shipped over by plane. It's the sort of intuition we can't turn on or off. When we know, we really know. It just kicks in automatically.

A sport utility parks next to my car in the parking lot of the Dayton's Mens and Home Store. It carries three adopted Korean kids and their parents. The eldest, a girl about seven or eight, walks the closest to her father as they head toward the store entrance. She reminds me of myself, even at twenty-five. She is her father's favorite and she knows it. She takes big steps to keep up with his deliberate small ones. He is her hero, her idol. She takes notes on the way he walks and tries to copy him, attempting to take the same long strides. She observes his facial expressions and the tone in his voice. She falls behind him, at which he calls over his shoulder, "Anna, this way, hon."

I study them. The father has features of Norwegian and German ancestry. He could be anyone's father growing up in the suburbs of Minneapolis, cleaning a garage, mowing a lawn, going fishing, watching football on Monday evenings, barbecuing on the grill in the summertime. His daughter does not look like anyone's daughter growing up in the suburbs of Minneapolis.

* *China* means "Chinese girl" in Spanish. It is used to refer to a person of Asian descent.

Everything about this father/daughter relationship appears normal. However, when she is my age, society, even Minnesota society with all its adopted Koreans, will not find them so normal looking. When she is much older and her father says to her in public, "Anna, this way hon," when she falls behind him, they simply will not appear so normal.

I never felt entirely comfortable studying race, class and gender in college. I felt naive when professors talked about contexualizing and intellectualizing all the "isms". It seemed every problem, particularly with race, had a theoretical answer. "Turn to page 241," in your textbook, the white Women's Studies professor said, "read Amy Tan or Alice Walker," the white English professor said. Okay, I said. I have to admit, at times it gave me comfort. Suddenly I could intellectualize why I experienced racism. Finally there were reasons why all the kids called me names and spit at me and why I didn't have any friends. I could read about why and how it was my experiences changed and transformed from a little girl to a young woman in college and then in the "real" world, which I am told by my conservative Republican father, I presently inhabit. Any problem I had that had to do with my race, I could intellectualize with the best of them. There I was, a college senior, accepted into a Ph.D. level, literary criticism class of "ethnic women's writing". Unfortunately, the course was canceled because not enough graduate students applied, but I kept the textbooks required for the class and studied them religiously. Just in case.

When I was at a "real world" party last weekend, a 35th birthday celebration for one of the accountants in the corporation I work for and in walked a stripper, I quickly consulted all those academic resources I'd read in college. My face and throat burned. I didn't know what to do. I thought of essays in "Transforming a Rape Culture", essays by Andrea Dworkin, Bell Hooks and all of my *Ms.* Magazines, but nothing came to mind. I was surrounded by about one hundred colleagues (including my bosses) and their significant others and I appeared to be the only one troubled by what I saw. When feminist theory couldn't save me, I left. I came to the conclusion quickly that it wasn't an appropriate time to stand on a chair and recite Adrienne Rich. It was better that I leave and show that I was not about to watch. Nobody noticed my exit. They were too busy watching the "entertainment".

I stood alone on the deck of the house overlooking Lake Minnetonka. When the stripper finally finished, smokers began to file outside. It was a beautiful night. The moon was almost full, falling on the surface of the water. Latin music came from inside the house, sounds of the Dominican Republic. And then I heard it. A white woman standing about thirty feet away who I had never met, let alone seen before, proclaimed, "I don't mind Latin Americans, but those Orientals really bug me." Immediately, a herd of ants came to mind, the way hundreds of them move around in such an organized fashion, secretly working together, making houses, bringing in food for their young. Once again, I looked inward, searched for something by Maxine Hong Kingston, Jessica Hagedorn or Janice Mirikitani to save me. But my face and throat still burned. All I wanted to do was kick her ass.

As I walked toward the woman to verbally confront her, my beautiful Latina friend, Josefina, rushed over to my side, her soothing low voice a bit shaken. "I heard what that woman said," she told me. "You don't have to say anything to her. It isn't your job."

Later that evening, when a large circle of us danced, I noticed that the woman who made the comment about Orientals had positioned herself in the room so she faced me. She glared at me with a knowing grin. How did an Oriental get on the guest list of this exclusive party, was what she may have well just said. I danced with one of my bosses, Armando, from Argentina. She can tolerate Armando but I bug her, was all I could think. And then I imagined ants again, lots of them, hidden in the corners of the room where nobody can see.

When colleagues and planning committees found out I was seeing Alek, a stockbroker in the same corporation, he began receiving invitations addressed to him with my name written below his. He is in upper management. I am not in upper management, but I

75

doubt my name would have been written next to his, even if I was. The only time I wasn't invited to a function with him, was at his going away party recently which was a "men only" function. The morning after, he told me it was the most fun he'd had in a long time, that it reminded him of an old fraternity outing in his Ivy League days. "Men can relax when their wives aren't around, you know how it is, Karita," he said. My first thought was, he's not perfect, but then, who is? My second thought was, what the hell am I doing with him? At the time, I didn't want to think about the answers to the question.

Alek had not come to the birthday party that evening for the accountant. He was supposed to be on a plane headed for his new home of two years, Madrid, Spain. We'd said our good-byes the evening before, which basically amounted to his saying, "I don't do goodbyes very well, so I simply don't do them."

"Me either," I replied.

While the Latin dancing at the party continued, many men stood around and watched, some of whom were Latin American them- selves. I recall, even the most "progressive" professors I encoun- tered in academia, believed that everyone in "third world" coun- tries is oppressed, victimized and needs charitable Americans to rescue them and tell them how to live their lives. They didn't real- ize they were contributing to the stereotypes about "third world" people. In Latin America, the more upper class the individual, the more Caucasian they often appear. Fact is, no matter what coun- try one travels to, there is always old money and good ol' boys running the show. There were so many men standing around who looked as if they'd just come from the golf course, I thought I was standing in my parents' house on a Sunday afternoon. Sunday, since I've been a little girl, is the day of the week my par- ents start their perfectly lovely morning off with brunch at the country club where my father is a member and then enjoy a day of golf with his business associates and their families.

Toward the end of the merangue with Armando, I glanced behind me at the row of fresh-faced boys in their Ralph Lauren V- neck sweaters, Sulka shirts, pressed chinos and Italian loafers and spotted Alek. He had been watching me. With a private grin, he put his hand up and waved. He mouthed what looked like, "Plane was delayed." He motioned for me to come over.

I never told him what the woman said about Orientals. Just like I never told him much about the blatant and "subtle" racism I've encountered in my life. My sister, who, like my brother, is biologically my parents' daughter, once made a comment at a family dinner while Alek was present. I'd asked who had cut her hair and she replied nonchalantly, "Oh, this stupid little Vietnamese girl." She had no idea why I would ever be offended by such a comment. Later, Alek said to me, "Your sister seems a bit naive about the world, about a lot of things, actually." I simply agreed with him. He knew there was nothing he could say that would matter or mean anything. After all, not everything needs to be critiqued, intellectualized or requires an answer. It's fine simply to feel hurt and angry.

In truth, I've known all along what it is I'm doing with Alek. When I first met him, it was as if we'd known one another most of our lives and had just spoken yesterday. There was a familiar feeling with him that I find rare in most people I know, even those who presently inhabit my personal life. He has no roots. He's never lived in more than one place for four years. He doesn't know his parents. They sent him away to boarding schools as a small child and he went to prep school and college in Massachusetts, immediately after. His father is Russian, his mother is blue-blood American and he was born and raised in Colombia. I know what that feels like. We've never discussed it in great detail. When you know the intimate details of a person's interior life, there is so much that seems trivial to discuss. In fact, when we were together, we never said much. We had a rhythm to our companionship that I've often observed in old, married people, like my grandparents. The kind that go to lunch on weekday afternoons, sit across from one another and say nothing. It's comforting somehow.

Carlos, a colleague of Alek's, invited us over for dinner one evening. I had met him and his wife, Flavia, both from Peru, once or twice before at parties, but had never gotten to know them. I'd first met Flavia at a private "tea" for the wives and significant others of businessmen in the corporation. My boss said I'd been invited to help translate for some of the Spanish speaking wives whose English was not yet proficient. But I knew it was because of my association with Alek. The women who had organized the party had probably wanted to test my "trophy wife" skills at such a function. In any case, it was hardly the time to really get to know anyone personally.

Carlos and Flavia were genuinely warm toward me, excited that they finally had gotten a chance to have me over to their house. I felt comfortable around them right away, which is why it startled me when I heard Carlos call Flavia, "China". I thought I'd heard him wrong. Only I heard it again and again. When Alek and Carlos were discussing the latest edition of the Financial Executive Journal, I excused myself and joined Flavia in the kitchen to get to the bottom of it.

"Why does he call you China?" I asked in Spanish.

"It's his nickname for me," she answered, "because my eyes go like this when I smile." She demonstrated by pulling her eyes back with her index fingers, giving her eyes the slant that so many kids had done to me, deliberately making fun of my "slanted chink eyes." It was so startling to see again after all those years, I didn't know what to say.

"But it's so derogatory!" I finally replied.

"No, no it's not," she said matter of factly, obviously unaware that I was taking it personally.

"But I would be offended, very offended if someone called me a China."

"But it's how someone calls someone a China. If I yell at you "China! You are this, or China! You are that, or China! Go back to where you come from! That would be an insult. But we have friends in Lima who are Japanese and we call them Chino and

China when we talk about them, because they like it, it's their nicknames. We call them these names as a term of endearment. But now that we know you don't like it, we will never call you it," she assured me.

I still felt rather uneasy about it.

A time I felt equally uneasy was when Alek and I had dinner at a Korean restaurant. It was early in our friendship, when I didn't know him as well. We had been discussing the kind of food we liked and when I mentioned that I was beginning to like Korean food, he suggested we go. Our waitress, the same waitress I'd had the other few times I'd eaten there, looked at me with suspicion when Alek and I walked in together. She had been unusually patronizing toward me in the past. I figured she probably had adopted Korean radar as well. Perhaps it wasn't only an adopted Korean phenomenon. I've heard that Korean immigrants, no matter what generation, tend to look down on Korean adoptees. I don't want to assume all Koreans are like this, but the few experiences I've had with them, first, second and third generation, have not been exactly positive.

What I noticed about Alek was that, unlike many white people I've taken to Korean restaurants, he didn't feel a need to mention every Korean person he knew, or what Asian countries he'd traveled to, or everything he knew about Asia. Our conversations revolved around the usual. He also seemed comfortable around me, as usual. However, I reeked of discomfort. I felt particularly self-conscious when I realized the waitress had talked with the other women working, about us. After awhile, four women stood behind the cash register and gawked at us. I had no idea what they were saying and couldn't read their facial expressions or the tone in their voices. I was relieved that Alek was facing the window.

After dinner, he went to get his car and I went to the register to pay. The women who had been gawking at us throughout dinner met me at the register and began bombarding me with comments and questions. "Your boyfriend is so handsome! So tall! Athletic build! Good teeth! Nice dresser! Is he rich? What does he do for a living? He is the best looking American we've ever seen with a Korean girl! You're adopted Korean?! Oh well, it's okay! Look at your boyfriend! So nice!"

I was embarrassed. I had seen other white men in the restaurant that evening with Asian women. It was clear to me these Korean women thought I was "lucky" not only to be with a white man, but a white man who looked and carried himself like Alek. I also was startled. I hadn't realized until then that the things they'd said about Alek, were the same things women (mostly friends of my mother or complete strangers) had been saying about my brother, most of his adult life. Physically being with Alek always felt so familiar and natural to me. It made me aware of yet another complexity that adopted Koreans face when dealing with the people we choose to date or marry.

"You ever notice how it's always the geeky, weird white guys that are with Asian women?" My friend Rachel, also an adopted Korean, mentioned. "The worst part is, you get the feeling a lot of these women are just with the guy because he's white. Either way you look at it, it's gross. And yet, look at me, who am I to point fingers? I've never personally known any Asian American guys. My whole family is white. Every guy I've ever dated is white. What am I supposed to do about it?"

Later, when Alek and I were getting to know one another better, he told me he knew how uncomfortable I'd been at the Korean restaurant with him. His depth in understanding my discomfort surprised me. "I've often tried to imagine just how different my life would have been if I'd been raised primarily in Russia or America or anywhere else for that matter. I think about the food, the people, the language, the lifestyle. I know I would have even felt different about myself. When I first moved to Massachusetts, I felt like a foreigner, but on a level that none of the other international students in prep school or college could grasp. They had been born and raised in one country--the country that their parents were also from. They belonged to that country and felt connected to it on a level that I never could about any of the countries or states I've lived in. They didn't know how it felt to always have this displaced feeling, this feeling that I never really belong anywhere. Every now and then I'll hear a language I don't know and my first reaction is, 'I could have spoken that language. I could have grown up in that culture instead of this one or that one or the other.' I recall that it's always been such a lonely feeling, no matter how old I am or where I am. It's just very lonely. Do you know what I'm talking about?" he asked.

"I'm afraid so," I answered.

A few days before Alek boarded the plane that was supposed to take him to Madrid, the movers had come to pack his belongings. A representative from the corporation, a woman who appeared to be in her early fifties, stopped by to tie up loose ends with the movers. She took one look at me and I could see it in her eyes. What is he doing with her? He can do so much better. I am certain she would have given the same look to most women, no matter what their race or physical appearance. It has always been expected that Alek "marry well" and nobody in the corporation thinks of a Minnesota woman of any persuasion as particularly good stock. However, I do know it startled her to see an Oriental. I also think she was surprised to see someone ten years younger than him. She struck up a conversation with Alek about Europe, her husband and their friends who have homes in France and Italy and who collect art. She positioned herself so that I was not a part of their conversation. Alek attempted to move, so I could be a part of it, but somehow she moved again so it looked as if I was standing in the background.

"What are you going to do with your toy?" she asked, referring to his Italian sports car.

"Sell it," he answered.

"Of course you are," she said, looking over her shoulder at me.

"There comes a time when we all have to grow up, find a car that suits our lifestyle a bit more, don't we?"

The TV was on. The movers watched the sports channel. The

stockmarket moved across the bottom of the screen. Alek had his TV programmed so he can watch the stockmarket. It's not as if he really watches, he has it on continuously for the same reason most people have a TV or radio on in the background. I never was able to completely tune it out and learned after awhile, neither was he. When we used to leave work together, go to his house for lunch, there it was: the stockmarket. Often, someone would call and interrupt our lunch. He could always tell the person what prices and shares and commodities he'd just seen. It always amazed me, because I knew he had been paying attention to our conversations. And at night, in his sleep he would mumble numbers, talk about them dropping. Once, he jumped out of bed so far, that he fell on the floor.

When the representative finally left and the movers were outside, Alek and I packed his carry-on, to take with him on the plane. The stockmarket was in the background, bells ringing and chaos. We were both crying, just barely and we were not looking at one another.

"You're running again," I said, handing him his watch, already set on Madrid time.

"Deep down, I think you're a bit relieved," he answered.

I was in line at the grocery store today. There was a woman behind me, her groceries overflowing from her cart. It struck me how tired she looked, how very tired and yet, I imagine there isn't a day that goes by when she doesn't look like this. Still, she looked pleasantly satisfied about something in her life that I haven't figured out yet in my own. Her movements were rehearsed, the way she unloaded her groceries. All the food she bought was non-perishable. There was nothing fresh, no produce, no meat besides pounds of hamburger in bulk. She had bottles of generic laundry detergent and shampoo for kids. Half her cart was filled with peanut butter and strawberry jam. She had coupons sticking out of her wallets but no grocery list.

Somehow, I think Alek inherently understood how profound the affect my inter-racial adoption has had in so many facets of my life, continues to have and always will. His understanding reached further than many whites and Asian Americans I've known, no matter what their level of education. The first time he met me, he really saw me. He saw what so many of us never actually see or look for in the people we've known, much of our lives. He didn't need to prove to me how much he knew or what he assumed or didn't assume. He was not someone who projected "guilt" for being white, or was careful not to say the "right" or "wrong" things. He realized over time, that it's not the blatant racism I encounter that hurts me most. It's the day-to-day things. The family things. The internal things. Things that wear an adopted Korean down over a long stretch of time. Things that put us through test after test after test. I think it was his knowing, that always gave me such comfort.

I can imagine what he would have thought about the woman in line behind me. "She's very lucky," he would say, "and I don't think she even knows it."

"Yes, she's very lucky," I would answer.

# From the Eyes of a Real Asian Man
## (on Korean adopted females)

### Beth Kyong Lo

*tramp*
*whore*
*slut*

You know the type

The kind who
hangs at smoky pool halls
late night, sipping beer
and hitting bud.
Creating panic
in fairy tale homes
where mom and dad
can't understand
why she wants
to leave so bad.

The kind who runs away
to live among boys
with itchy fingers
aching to be pleased,
who don't say no,
never say no
laying still under
sweaty bed covers
with no moans, no aches
just a body of pleasure.

*can't cook*
*can't clean*
*can't eat right*

You know the type
the kind who wants

to be down with you
and are willing
to do anything
to prove themselves;
bad girls yearning to be good,
but can't.  Not like the real
Asian butterflies.

*too loud*
*too domineering*
*not respectful enough*

American girls
we want to fuck
like we'd never do
to a proper Asian born,
Asian raised girl
who pushes away
puckered lips and spits
in sexual faces.
Only in heaven
can we have the American slut
with desirable rice eyes.

Queens of rejection
half breeds
ugly stuck up
Americanized
gaping pussies,

>　*Are you like that Korean adopted chick, Linda?*

You know
the one who knows
Vietnamese
Hmong
and Lao bad boys,
sucking cock and kissing ass.
You know--
>　　　they are all alike.

# *Laurel*

## *YoungHee*

I obsess. My obsessing is highly ritualized. It is meticulous and never ending. There are times when it takes over, controls my behavior to a point that I feel no lightness, no joy, and no relief. I obsess over white women. I compare every inch of my body to theirs. I hate them and worship them at the same time. I feel guilty that my obsessing objectifies other women. I am ashamed that I value myself in vain ways. I detest the narcissism in my thought patterns.

I used to believe I was white. At least I was completely emotionally invested in this belief. Theoretically I was white, my family is white, the community I grew up in was white, and I could not point out Korea on a map, nor did I care about such a place. The only thing I heard about Korea was that they ate dogs. I denied that I was Korean to everyone, most painfully, I denied it to myself.

However, my image staring back at me in the mirror betrayed such a belief. There I saw it, the rude and awful truth...slanted-hooded eyes, non-existent eyelashes, "yellow" skin, short legs, and long torso. I hated myself, this betrayal, being given such a look without any knowledge of where it came from.

From a very young age, I constantly compared my body proportions to other white women. I suppose all women do the same, given our culture's obsession of how one should look. I compare like no other. Race gives this unspoken competition a slightly different slant because of the power relations at work. Unfortunately, many white women look at other white women and experience envy. Indeed, this is the nature of institutionalized sexist culture. But to desire to be an entirely different race is a deep-seated, painful need--a need that is full of shame and inexplicable guilt.

The first woman I ever obsessed about was named Laurel. Laurel was my best friend in high school. She epitomized all I desired to be but was not. She had blond hair, blue eyes, big breasts, long legs, and an awareness of how she affected everyone around her. This knowledge gave her uncanny confidence. She manipulated her position of desirability by expressing her sexuality freely and without shame to many different people. I watched her. I constantly compared myself to her. She fascinated me. I was invisible next to her, people talked to me to get a hold of any information they could about her. I existed only as a vehicle for others to get close to Laurel. Through others' obsessions with Laurel, I, too, became obsessed. Every weekend, I would either stay at her house or she would sleep at mine. Laurel was very sexually experienced and would tell me what sex was like. I remember her describing the smell, the taste of sex, and how it felt. We were only high school girls, but she had already had many lovers. She was the only human that ever told me I was pretty, smart, and was capable. For many weeks during these sleep-overs, we would lie in bed together and she would talk and I would listen, watch her, smell her, want to touch her. I wanted something beautiful for myself. I wanted to touch perfection. Inevitably, my relationship with her became sexual. I was not particularly attracted to her, but sex was the easiest way to explore my obsession. Our lovemaking was more of a mantra of how much I wished I was like her. I fucked her because I wanted to be her. I hated myself perhaps the most, during our lovemaking. I worshipped her. I saw the way my body looked laying next to her and felt so ashamed to be Asian. My body seemed far too small, almost pathetically unwomanly. And then when I thought I could bear it no longer, I would compare once more.

Internalized oppression is something I still struggle with to this day. At least now I have a language to write about it in, clear reason of why I felt so inferior to Laurel. I have wanted to write about her for a long time. To this day, this particular experience haunts me like no other. With every new relationship I enter, I confess my story about Laurel. I am not sure why. Perhaps I am warning my new lover that their desire for a certain type of person would be devastating. Of course such a desire is always present. I think my relationship with Laurel made such a lasting impression on me because she allowed me to realize my position in this culture. By witnessing the power she enjoyed, it forced me to realize that although I felt "white," I could never experience that kind of privilege and power white people enjoy. The world saw me as different, "othered" and that is when I started to see myself more clearly. I was not proud to be Asian American. I hated other Asians because they forced me to see myself in them.

White people are often shocked or somewhat horrified that I could envy or want white features. I am bemused that they have such a hard time understanding why this is. I was not born with shame. I learned shame through countless experiences. By the time I was twelve, I knew looking a certain way was more valued. I learned the desire to be white from white culture.

Being adopted into a white family does give one a unique perspective.

In a way, I am more a part, more comfortable around white people than many of my other friends of color. I no longer believe I am white, but I still have days when I desire to look white. Those days are difficult and painful. I still do not know what it means to be Korean American, but I do have a sense of what it means to be Asian American. I no longer fear other Asians, but am ravenous for their company. I now have the intellectual skills to problematize, theorize, and understand the complexities of identity politics. This gives me agency. I have had relationships with women similar to the one I have described, but none of them stay with me as she does.

I ended up not being able to be around Laurel after our relationship became sexual. I often think of her. Writing this essay gives me some kind of closure with her.

# Prayer At The Walls

## Grant Barnes

*for Miki Kim and Greg Louganis*

Now there is the silence of every blank page;
there is the silence of writing before knowing,
the knowing of one's own history as it was;
there is the silence of witnessing, always
the spinning wheels, and there is also always
the silence of poetry that is too short for me.

And that silence is strong that comes like so:
always told to wear shoes that were so tight
that the having to wear them was like a hurt
beyond crying, and I thought that living well
was being able, on one's own, to seize upon
one shoe's tongue, take it out, so make room.

There has been the silence of the holding in,
and of the waiting, the silence of the phone,
when its ringing isn't answered, the silence
of the crying out loud, as my speech is erased,
and the silence of imagining celebration, and
the silence of impediments which are blessed.

I write of the repetition that is language's way
of recreating silence, of writing which is that
repetition, and of silences which are repetitions,
for then everything had to be told, told to him,
told to get attention, intimacy renewing walls:
after you stay alive once, you stay alive again.

    Father, my Father, forgive you me,
    for you know not what I must do--
    must use my sex to excite only that
    which was the quiet violence you gave

--you know not how to forgive me.

I write now as an old blind cat, wild and mean,
giving birth most quietly in some hidden place,
hardly even knowing I was somehow pregnant,
and I write also as a blind new kitten, one found
in a tight old shoe, not knowing if I'll be alive
tomorrow, but today newly beginning to stir--
this animal scratching still on the old walls of
my secret annex, in my own violent fondling.

The walls of Jericho the shoe must now seem,
holding back demons and monsters in defense,
invisibly speaking down to me, as if accepting
my silence but not yet my place which I in my
full-on terror face to bear witness, writing myself
a badly cast redemptive role, in the only sounds
he wouldn't hear-- the transgression of the walls,
looking at that leathery tongue, long discarded,
to find the self I won't but know when it's there.

# What Isn't Mine

## Eun Jung Che

So alone I sit resting against my pillows
Already anticipating the pain of missing
      you, because we are temporary
         Because permanence knows no home in this body
   And I will drift my whole life long.

So slowly
   I say goodbye to you and
         listen for the sounds of your departure
   The packing away of feelings and years
   And nothing I can do can stop you.
You leave because you must
Because no one can long for me
   Love knows time in my home
   It arrives and leaves
      and you, too, must go
And I must always love what isn't mine

I watch you intently
      Saying slowly words of farewell
      Speaking my tears
   Until you disappear from sight
   And I no longer know you

You, who created my sky and possessed my heart,
You are trying to love a ghost
      I am just a spirit, not really here
      a phantasm, fool's gold
   You will slide through me
      Sifting through years of wounds
      Searching for me under skin thick with scars
   And I cannot feel your hands because my skin
      has long since grown numb

But I commend the intention
I understand
   the depth of your sincerity
   as you promise me future promises
      that will be left undone
And we make our plans to fulfill your
   need to do what's right
As I say goodbye to you every time we make love
Recording the feeling of you inside of me
   as you create the hollowness
   that will ache with false feeling
The amputated limb of phantom pains
and we move quietly towards death

# Exchange

## Jo Rankin

Born unto two
Realities, two cultures: too different.
You and me,
Crying silent tears while attempting to
Exchange American branches for
Korean roots.
Is it possible?
Maybe.

# In America

*Leah Sieck*

In America

My Korean face
floats in the mirror:

Half-moon eyes,
proud cheekbones,
melon lips,
night black hair

haunt me.

If I could break the code,
the secrets of my genes
could take me back
to those first breaths--

Those seven days
when I was my true mother's
daughter
could tell me

if it is her face
I see.

Indianapolis, Indiana  1990

# Homeless

## Leah Sieck

*Mother,*
*Why did you leave me?*
*Where is my birthplace?*
*How can I come home?*

In Korea,
my return
is an infant's first
drawn breath

Being is
a stifled cry --
a longing for respite.

In the subway,
people sweep in and out
pushing me aside.
They are startled
when I don't speak their language

Among my Korean friends,
I retreat
from their circle of comraderie
My heart wants to speak
but my mouth cannot translate

*Mother,*
*Why did you leave me?*

Alone,
my hands trap my heart
as it seizes and trembles --
trying to escape
from its cage.

*Where is my birthplace?*

How many times to suffer
loss of origin
loss of mother tongue,
loss of being.

I long
for the comforting mirror
of your face.  I imagine
the eternal loving
touch -- the knowing
of your body

*How can I come home?*

I have journeyed so far.  Sacrificed
love and community to rediscover
my heritage
Yet
here,

the faces do not see
my difference.  They cannot
soothe the primal wound.
They cannot
heal me.

Why do I linger? --
for the ghost of you?

*Mother,*
*Why did you leave me?*
*Where is my birthplace?*
*How can I come home?*

Seoul, Korea   November 1996

# Living in Half Tones

*excerpt*

## Me-K. Ahn

When Rose awoke the next day, an immediate heaviness over-whelmed her, a sadness slowed her. She had been at the orphan-age in Chechon, Korea, for almost a week. A vague memory of images and sounds clouded her thoughts, creating a dull ache in her body.

The face of the orphanage director, June, flashed through her mind. An aging, wrinkled, reddened face. *Birth mother. Mother. Dead. Probably dead.* Rose glanced over at her adoptive mother, Nobuko, sleeping peacefully in the other twin bed. Her mouth was slightly open, her breathing heavy, textured with a raspy hoarseness. The soft, golden skin of her cheeks expanded and contracted with each breath. She sucked on her teeth, occasionally creating a high-pitched squeak like a baby's mouth on its mother's nipple. *Mother. Birth mother. Probably dead. Dead.*

While Rose lay in bed unable to move, her eyes began to swell with tears. Nobuko's voice returned again, insisting that she stop crying. Arthur, Rose's father, would have tried his damnedest to inhale all his tears, and Nobuko would have made fun of him. The relentless voice played over and over again, but this time Rose did not listen. She let the tears roll down her cheeks off her jawline onto the edge of the blue pillowcase. She didn't care if Nobuko said that she was only thinking of herself, or claim that the crying wouldn't help. This was her time to be selfish, and the warm wetness of the salty substance did make her feel better.

Nobuko began to roll around underneath the sheets. Five minutes later she woke up and began to dress. Rose tried to turn around but her arms and legs felt numb. She closed her eyes pretending to sleep. Nobuko went out to the balcony to smoke.

*Birth mother.*

*Mother.*
*Dead.*
*Probably.*

After lying in bed for another hour, Rose forced herself to get up and dress. As she began moving around the flat, the stale, suffocating air implored her to leave the orphanage for some fresh, rural, Chechon air. She walked outside and slowly descended the gravel driveway, dragging her white tennis shoes over the chalk-colored pebbles. Everything was bursting with moisture. The air waited anxiously for an inevitable shower, the leaves were sweating in the early morning sun, and the rice paddies sprayed mist in the light fragrant wind. It was like walking into a sauna where a thin coat of wetness immediately slapped itself onto your skin. Rose took a deep breath trying to absorb as much of the surrounding green lushness. As she continued to walk towards the mountains, she felt her skin expand with moisture.

The morning was quiet in its stillness, the sun diffused by thin, wispy cirrus clouds. Rose stopped to look around. She saw a large plateau in the misty distance and began walking faster towards the steep hill. A path, partly paved, led her to the top, and, once there, out of breath, she marveled at the panoramic view. Losing herself in the greenness, she continued towards the center of the plateau and came upon three large mounds equally spaced apart. Perfectly shaped, grass-covered spheres swelled from the earth. *Was it earth, air or water buried inside, or something entirely unearthly?*

*Birth mother.*
*Mother.*

Rose began to think of her birth mother. And the news that she was dead. Probably. It was odd to think about. Rose had always thought of Nobuko as her mother. She knew that she had not come from her womb, but rarely did she think of where she had spent the first nine months after conception. Korea had been a place that until now existed in outer space. And Rose was mysteriously conceived in that same space. She was not normal. It had not been an immaculate conception but a miraculous one.

But now, the woman who supposedly birthed her and left her was dead. A woman she had never known. A birth mother that had never before existed. She was introduced and then taken away at the same time.

She continued looking at the mysterious mounds that faced the large mountain range. A wooden sign etched in *hangul* stood in front of each grass sphere. A bird flew overhead, landing on the third mound.

Intellectually Rose knew what being adopted meant, but in her heart it was an abstract concept that held little meaning. It didn't relate to her. It had been easy for her to think that she wasn't adopted at all, that she hadn't any losses to grieve over. Arthur and Nobuko never spoke about a birth family or birth anything, trying to create a mirage that they were a family-by-birth. They never talked about abandonment, an orphanage or anything of her life before the adoption. They forgot to remember. It was always a given that her life had, indeed, started with them. She accepted this assumption with the innocence of her young mind.

It was easy for this mythical picture of a family to persist. Nobuko was Japanese. Rose's Korean features resembled hers. She was the "real" mother. Nobody else could claim Rose as their daughter. Arthur was white. He made their family more acceptable.

Rose moved closer to the wooden signs. She opened her black leather hip sack and pulled out a piece of paper and a pen. She slowly copied down the engraved hangul as carefully and accurately as she could. As she walked back towards the orphanage, she saw a patch of crimson flowers. She gazed at them for a moment, then reached down and plucked three of them out of the ground.

The children in the orphanage continued their daily routines. Breakfast at 8 a.m. Devotionals at 9 a.m. Playtime outside at 10 a.m. Lunch at noon and naps at 1 p.m. Baths at 3 p.m. More devotionals at 4 p.m. Dinner at 5. Playtime at 6 and bedtime at

7:30.

Later that evening, June and Rose were watching Korean television. They made small talk back and forth. Rose kept asking June what was happening on the 19" screen. June would try to explain, but Rose still could not understand. After the late night movie ended, June began surfing through the channels. The U.S. military channel AFKN flashed on and Rose recognized Jay Leno. English pulsing through the Korean airwaves caught her attention. June quickly flipped past it. Rose asked her to turn it back. Jay introduced a comic named Henry Lee.

"Hmmm," June said. "Lee. Maybe he's Korean."

A medium-sized, young Korean man with long, spiky hair walked onto the stage. The applause was hesitant, but his smile was automatic, spontaneous.

"Ever seen him?" June asked.

Rose shook her head no.    "I've heard his name before."

"Oh, I've never heard of him," June said while turning down the volume.

Rose continued to listen.

*"Hey, my name's Henry Lee. As you can probably tell by now, I'm Korean. I don't have a store or anything..."*   Restrained laughter from the audience.  *"Well, not anymore."*

June wanted to talk. Her mood had turned serious, pensive. "Now Rose, do you know why your parents adopted?"

"My mom tells me that she couldn't have children," she said while still looking at the television.

"Do you know why she couldn't?"

"No. She never talks about that. She just says that she couldn't."

*"I guess you're probably wondering about my accent. I grew up in Tennessee. Yep, that explains the southern drawl."* His self-deprecating tone reminded Rose of her brother, Bill.

"How did your parents meet?" June asked.

Rose shifted around on the couch. "They met in Japan when my dad was stationed in the army."

"Did they meet on the base?"

"I don't know. They may have. They don't talk about that either."

June leaned forward, resting her elbows on her knees. "Well, you know, I thought it was kind of unusual because every time I would go back to the States, we would call them, you know, to come to our little gatherings. And they never showed any interest at all. Did you ever know about this?"

"No, I've never heard anything about that."

"So, I've always wondered about them. I've always had this weird feeling."

*"What? You don't believe me. Can't imagine an Asian in the South. Scary thought, huh? Well, I was the only one, ya know. Me and my family. The only ones in Tennessee."*

"Have you had problems with your mom?" June continued.

"Well, you know, it's been hard, but we've made it through. It's been a lot better since I finished college. They give me a lot more freedom now. But it was pretty bad before that." Rose's eyes shifted back and forth to the television.

"Yeah, it is different that she's Japanese. I mean, I just hope...I hope that she treats you o.k."

"Treats me o.k.?"

"Well, there are a lot of problems between the Koreans and Japanese. They have a long history of treating the Koreans real bad."

"Yeah, actually a friend of mine told me about this recently. I felt really stupid because I had no idea. She couldn't believe that I didn't know. But, again, my mom never talks about it."

"Well, what about all this Japanese stuff anyway? I mean did she raise you that way or what?"

Rose paused a while to think. "Well, if you consider the food, the Buddhism and all that, I guess she did. But then again, I feel like they were raising me to be white because Mom was going through her own assimilation process. When I think about it, it's really confusing, but I think she was confused, too."

*"I'll never forget when we went to Korea for the first time and, look at me, do you think I even speak a word of Korean?"* He tries a few words pathetically. *"It was weird not being able to talk to anyone there."*

June leaned back on the couch. "Did she speak Japanese in the house?"

"Yeah, but only to her friends. She wanted to teach us but then claims that she thought we would get confused about speaking Japanese or English."

"And you say you never went to those Korean camps or anything."

"Oh, absolutely not," Rose said turning back toward the T.V.

"Why do you think your parents never talked about adoption?"

"Any time I bring it up, they get all nervous. It doesn't make sense since they were the ones who decided to adopt. I always knew I was adopted, but they never talked about Korea or anything. It was like they were scared of it."

"How did you find out you were adopted then?"

Rose paused again. "They must have just told me."

"So you don't remember?"

"No, I guess not. Well, wait. Let me think.... God, you know, it must have been because I went with them to pick Bill up at the airport when he first arrived. So I knew that was part of being adopted and that he didn't come from Mom's stomach. I probably thought he came from Chicago, too."

June gave her a puzzled look. "Chicago?"

"Yeah," Rose said with a slight smile, "I thought I was from Chicago, because my parents picked me up there."

"They didn't tell you you were from Korea?"

"I'm sure they did, but I guess I didn't know what that meant." Rose shifted in her seat and felt a little ball of stress forming inside her stomach.

*And man, you know, it was always easy to pick my father out from a crowd in Tennessee, but in Korea....I kept losing him."* More laughter.

"Sounds like maybe they were in denial."

"Denial?"

"Yeah, that you were even adopted. They were trying to make it seem like you were their 'real' kids."

Maybe that was true. Rose didn't know. She looked at June reaching for her glass of water. She focused on the glass and said, "Well, I felt like we were a real family.... Most of the time anyway."

June swallowed and said, "Why did you feel that?"

103

"It's just the way it was. Is there something wrong with that?" Rose felt herself getting defensive. The already uncomfortable edge in her voice was sharpening and her temperature began to rise.

June put her glass down. "It's hard to understand the whole thing, you know. It seems like you get along well enough and everything...but...have you ever talked about it with her?"

"Talked about what?"

"The Japanese thing."

The Japanese thing. Rose resisted the urge to remain silent. "I don't really know how to bring it up with her. I wouldn't know what to say."

"I'd just like to know what she was thinking. I mean why she wanted to adopt and all. You know it's funny. I had a say in some of the adoptions. Of course, the first priority was that the family was Christian. Something must have happened in your case."

Rose looked down at her bare feet and rubbed her toes together.

*"I got lost so many times and I would turn around and start talking to some guy who I thought was my father and he gave me the dirtiest look. Then I'd hear my father yelling for me, 'Heenn-lee, Henn-lee.' It was very embarrassing."*

"Do you know if your mom was a prostitute?"

Rose's face flushed a light red. The thought had never crossed her mind. "No...I don't think so...I mean...I can't imagine it."

"Well, the reason I ask is because a lot of times the prostitutes on the bases had so many abortions or miscarriages that they could-n't have babies anymore."

Rose didn't know what else to say. She had a strange feeling that June was searching for something negative. She continued to deny June's suspicions. But how did *she* know what was true?

"Was your mom's family poor? Because, you know, a lot of times the families had to sell their daughters into prostitution. They didn't have any other choice."

Rose's mind was spinning. She thought about Nobuko and Arthur's photo in the album. "Why don't you ask her? How am I supposed to know any of this. I told you, they don't tell me very much about their past."

"Now, Rose. I don't want to upset you, but don't you think it's all a little strange?"

Rose did not respond.

*"You know, I think the biggest advantage of being Asian in America is that you can pretend that you don't know how to speak English. If some-body asks you a dumb question, you can just look at them and say, 'Ahh, no-o-o speak-a Eng-rish.'"*

"And the other thing is, is that.... Now did your father ever sexually abuse you? I remember going back to the states one time and found out that one of my girls had been sexually abused by her father. I almost had a nervous breakdown when I found out about that. I couldn't deal with it. I felt so angry and guilty because I kept thinking, how did we let her go to that family? So, I just need to know."

Rose's body froze. She thought about Arthur. How friendly his smile had been, his quiet thoughtful nature, his gentle touch, his soft singing. "No, he never did anything like that," she said firm-ly.

# Unconventional Seoul

## Rebecca Smith

I always knew I was adopted. I don't recall the exact moment my parents told me. But I knew it made me different from others, almost as if I was born with a handicap. I was careful not to reveal that I had this affliction. It made me feel ashamed about myself. Nevertheless, I sometimes had a need to tell people. I wasn't some poor, illiterate from Asia. I was American. And I wanted to achieve what I thought that meant.

Growing up in a large Swedish community in the Midwest introduced me to the first criteria of what was considered the norm. Fair skin and blond hair were the standards I measured myself against. Honestly, I had no idea I didn't fit that description unless I saw my reflection in the mirror. I thought of myself as a Caucasian. What a shock to find out that I wasn't.

It was this revelation that convinced me that I was not a conventional person. How could I be? I was born to a woman I have never met. Not many people can brag about that. So I took that as a sign. I would either be very special or very unusual.

At the age of four, I discovered that being different was not the same as being special. Being taunted and teased by my peers was a rude awakening to how different I really was. But I could not blame my parents.

Instead, there were two other people who were responsible for my genetic makeup. The blame I placed onto them pacified my anger towards my dominant physical characteristics. Even though I have finally learned to accept myself, the struggle has been long and hard.

I always knew I was adopted. I don't recall any faces or names belonging to my biological parents. I don't even know if they are still alive. But I am certain of one thing. Their lives must have been very unusual as well.

# Tightrope

## David Miller

Walking a tightrope
Pulled on both sides
Korea
America
For if I fall either way
I lose a part of me.

*Reunions*

# What I Was Told

## K. Burdette

*What I Was Told*

I was born in Washington, D.C. to a Korean father and a (presumably white) American mother. My birthparents "didn't think they could take care of me" and so they put me up for adoption.

I was told nothing about my birthmother. But I once overheard my adoptive grandmother say that my birthmother had blonde hair and freckles and that I must have gotten my freckles from her.

I imagined having lots of blonde cousins.

*What I Presumed*

I presumed, as most adoptees do, that my parents were unmarried and that they were young--probably teenagers.

*What My Adoptive Parents Knew But Elected Not To Share With Me*

My father was a successful businessman, working on a graduate degree. He was an only child. He was married with two sons. My mother was one of his employees. She had long, blonde hair and green eyes. She came from a large family of German-Irish descent.

*What People Asked Me*

Where are you from?
Well, where were you born?
How come you have a French name when you look East Asian?

Are you from China or something?
How did you find out you were adopted?
Have you been to Korea?
Do you want to go to Korea?
Do you speak Korean?
Are you interested in Korean culture/history?
Do you know why your birthparents gave you up?
Do you want to meet your birthparents?


*Searching*

I started searching when I was 21--that's how old you have to be to sign up with some of the registries. I was advised by a search group to write a letter to the agency through which I was adopted. My letter received no response. Months later, I called the agency, and a meeting with a social worker was set up.


*What the Social Worker Told Me*

The social worker's name was Denise. In February, we met at the Prince George's County Department of Social Services. This is what she told me:

My mother grew up in Virginia. She was the youngest of six children. She enjoyed bowling, reading, and volunteer work. She was a high school graduate. She was 21 when I was born.

My father enjoyed golfing, bowling, tennis, chess, and fishing. He was described (by my mother) as a "very pleasant, well-rounded person who enjoys life very much." He sent my mother flowers every day she was in the hospital.

My mother named me "Emily Renea." I would have had her (Irish) surname.

The social worker informed me that the agency assisted with "limited reunion searches"--if I signed a notarized document, the agency would search for my birthparents and, if they agreed, set up a meeting. In August, she called me with the name, address, and phone number of my birthfather.

## Meeting My Father

I arranged to meet my father at a restaurant in Chinatown. I wore a plaid skirt, a black t-shirt, and black tights. I brought pictures of myself as a child.

He had white hair, glasses, and expensive clothes. He was shorter and stockier than I would have imagined.

We discovered a mutual admiration for John Garfield, Sterling Hayden, and Myrna Loy. He said that Jean Gabin was his favorite actor and that while growing up in Korea he'd had a crush on Danielle Darrieux. I told him that I preferred Arletty and Dita Parlo.

He told me (repeatedly) that I was nothing like my mother. He said that I was not what he'd expected. I asked what it was he had expected. He said, "I don't know...A regular kid from P.G. County who ate hamburgers."

The restaurant manager later asked a mutual acquaintance if the man I'd met that night had been a date.

## Meeting My Mother

My mother and I met at a seafood restaurant someone had recommended to her. We walked over to another restaurant, when we discovered that there was nothing vegetarian on the menu. I wore the same skirt I'd worn to meet my father and brought the same photographs.

She wore blue eyeshadow and gold jewelry. She was slightly overweight or "chubby", as my father had described her.

She told me the crooked pinkie fingers I had ran in her family.

We drove to a bookstore nearby. I asked what sort of books she liked to read. She told me she'd read anything but that she particularly liked reading history. No one would have imagined we were mother and daughter.

I saw her twice more.


*Films I've Seen With My Father*

*Sunrise*
*The Crying Game*
*Flirting*
*A Brief History of Time*
*Zentropa*
*Eat Drink Man Woman*
*La Traviata*
*Diabolique*
*Red*
*Children of Paradise*

The proprietor of the Georgetown restaurant my father and I frequent asks questions about me, my father, my mother. I try to answer his questions without revealing the peculiarity of our situation. My father's immediate family doesn't know I exist.


*My Grandmother*

The first time I met my father, he told me that I looked like his mother when she was my age. He said she was 4'11", she weighed about 80 pounds and that she walked incredibly fast--like I did.

I met my father's parents last year when I was in Los Angeles. The four of us went out to dinner.

My father thanked me for wearing a dress but jokingly complained about the hole in my tights. Throughout dinner, they spoke about me in Korean. Occasionally, I asked my father what they were talking about. My grandmother said she thought I was too skinny. She held my hand tightly.

My grandfather had had a stroke and wasn't terribly aware of what was going on.

After dinner, they showed me family photos. I'd never seen my father's wife before. My grandmother shoved a couple of hundred-dollar bills into my hand. I thanked her without counting them.

I returned to my grandparents' house the day before I left L.A. My grandmother understood the words "tomorrow" and "go". She poured me a V-8 and gave me more photo albums to look at. She shoved more bills into my hand. I took their photograph on the patio.

They wanted to take me to lunch but I had made plans with someone else. They walked me outside and waved goodbye until I disappeared from view.

My grandfather died shortly after my visit.


*Lately...*

I last spoke to my mother four years ago when I found out my ex-lover had moved in with the woman for whom he left me and couldn't reach any of my friends on the phone. She later told my father she felt bad she couldn't help me.

She did send me a Christmas present (a leather purse) through my father that year--but I don't carry a purse.

I last saw my father a day before my last birthday when we saw *Children of Paradise* at the National Gallery. I sent him a postcard of Jean Gabin and Michelle Morgan from Paris last month.

*\*This is a very slightly fictionalized account of the author's experiences. Details have been changed to protect the privacy of the writer's birthparents.*

115

# Remembering The Way Home:
## A Documentary Video Proposal
### excerpts

## Deann Borshay

*My brother looks like James Dean, my sister and mother wear Jackie O hairdos, my father holds a movie camera to his eye, wearing a dark suit, a thin tie and a smile. They greet me at the San Francisco International Airport and lead me to a blue Cadillac with white leather interior. We drive off to the manicured lawns of the California suburbs.*

*This is 1966 America--the Vietnam War, the Civil Rights Movement, flower power, radical social change combined with economic prosperity and optimism. I have just gotten off a 16-hour flight from an alien, dec - imated land, a land where people live in hovels with no indoor plumbing, running water, toilets, or modern conveniences, a land where women cannot feed their children, some forced to sell them. Through one long airplane ride, I have stepped out of and into a different historical epoch. I am eight years old.*

*Background*

In 1953 Harry Holt, an Oregon farmer, began a small-scale rescue operation of children orphaned as a result of the Korean War. His effort led to one of the largest and most efficient adoption agencies specializing in Korean children in the United States. In 1954, the Korean government established a special agency under the Ministry of Social Affairs to expedite the adoption of Amerasian children, mostly "illegitimate" offspring of American soldiers and Korean prostitutes, by families in the U.S. and other countries. This also paved the way for full-blooded Korean children to be adopted out efficiently at an unprecedented scale.

While the Korean War ended over 40 years ago and South Korea's economy and standard of living have vastly improved, the number of Korean children adopted by American families and other countries continued to increase through the 1980s. South Korea has been the largest supplier of children for adoption to developed countries in the world, with the peak in 1986 when over 6,200 Korean children were sent to the U.S. in a single year (with thousands also sent to Europe). Some estimate that 80,000 Korean children have been adopted by U.S. families; others estimate that the number is well over 100,000.

I was among the first wave of Korean orphans to be sent to America in the 1960s. *Remembering The Way Home* chronicles my struggle to reconcile the demands of two families, two cultures, and two nations, and to resolve a decades-long case of mistaken identity.

My parents signed up to support a girl named Cha Jung Hee through the Foster Parent's Plan. After sending $15 a month and clothes and letters to Cha Jung Hee for two years, they "fell in love with her", and decided to adopt her. In interviews, they describe their decision to adopt and the initial adjustment process for me and the family. Dad: "*In the beginning, people used to stare and look at us funny. They'd do a sort of double-take, you know, look once, then look again. The brave ones would then ask us, is she your daughter? and point to you. Then I would say, of course she is, we look just alike, don't we? (laughs).*"

Once I could speak English, I tried many times to explain to my American mother the truth about who I was: "*You adopted the wrong girl. I am not Cha Jung Hee.*"

My mother thought I was having "bad dreams" and reassured me by pointing to my adoption papers for proof about my background: I was Cha Jung Hee, no mother, no father, no relatives.

Being eight years old, however, I remembered a few things. I remembered visiting my father's grave. I remembered being carried on my brother's back to an orphanage and running away to see my mother. And I remembered the director of the orphanage saying to me on the way to the airport, "Don't tell them who you really are until you're old enough to take care of yourself," not fully understanding the meaning of his words.

Mom: "*The papers said you were Cha Jung Hee, it even said so on your passport. And I think it also said your dad died during the Korean War and your mom died giving birth to you. We had nothing else to go on.*"

The confusion and conflict between actual memories and the "facts" as written in my adoption documents became so great that I developed amnesia. I forgot everything about Korea: the name of the orphanage, the language, the fact that I had brothers and sisters, even my own name. Instead, I exerted all my energies in learning to become an American. I observed my parents, my American brother and sister, my new friends, characters on television, ads in magazines and began to imitate language, gestures, facial expressions, and forms of speech--all the qualities an American was supposed to have. I developed a persona that was fully American within the first year and by my senior year in high school, became head cheerleader, president of my class, honor student, homecoming queen.

The adjustment problems that never surfaced in those early years, along with the grieving over the loss of my Korean family, all came 15 years later, when I left home for college. The happy American facade that was characteristic of my high school years gave way to nightmares and incoherent dreams. What I thought to be memories started coming back from my childhood, vague memories of a family, a house, my father's death. As I began mourning the death of my father and the loss of my family, I became emotionally detached from my American family and friends and entered a deep depression.

For the first time, my relationship with my American parents entered a crisis period. While I was growing up, we never fought or argued. Now our relationship was filled with tension, anger, confusion, and regret. I became angry at them for having adopted me, for keeping my true identity from me, and for being so American. At the same time, my parents were at a loss as to what to do, wondering whether they had made a mistake in adopting me, trying to avoid discussing the adoption issue for fear that it would make things worse.

*Part 2*

*Dear Sun Duk Orphanage. My name is Cha Jung Hee. I was adopted by the Borshay family in America in 1966, but I think Cha Jung Hee is not my real name. I also believe I may still have family in Korea. Could you please tell me whether this is true or not, and whether I have family there?*

I wrote this letter in May, 1981. Six weeks later, I received a response:

*"My dear sister, you don't know how happy I am to write to you now. I am your brother Ho Jin. Mother, who used to think of you days and nights, is so happy to read your letter and to see the picture of you, she can't make good sleep at night. Your last name is Kang and your first name is Ok Jin. We are five brothers and sisters in our family. You are the fourth. I am certain you are Kang Ok Jin, not Cha Jung Hee."*

\* \* \*

Through his letters, my brother told me the story of how I came to America as Cha Jung Hee. In 1965, the Borshays signed the adoption papers for Cha Jung Hee and sent their money to Korea. Cha Jung Hee was ready to go to America. But at the last minute, Cha Jung Hee's mother had second thoughts and backed out of the deal. It was a desperate time in Korea, and the social worker at the orphanage did not want to waste the opportunity for one of her orphans to get a good American upbringing and education. She decided to send somebody else. Since I was about the same height and age as Cha Jung Hee, she decided to send me as Cha Jung Hee. My picture was pasted onto Cha Jung Hee's birth certificate and passport. When the director of the orphanage took me to the airport in Seoul one cold winter morning, his last words to me were: "Don't tell them who you really are until you're old enough to take care of yourself."

\* \* \*

A couple of years after I was sent to the U.S. in 1966, my brother and sister left the orphanage and went back to live with my mother. Their lives returned more or less to normal, somehow aided by my absence.  Gradually, their circumstances started improving. The family photos show weddings, births of new babies, and holiday celebrations through the 70s, 80s, and into the 90s.  We see my family moving from a one-room house with no hot water, no indoor bathroom, and no indoor kitchen to a modern apartment building, buying modern appliances, and eventually enjoying family vacations at the seaside.  Over the course of the past 30 years, they have graduated into a newly formed Korean middle class.

What is startling when I look at my Korean family pictures is that during the past 30 years, they have had a very full, productive life.  This is a disturbing and sad realization because I was not and am not a part of that life.  As I look at these photos, I can see the life I would have had with my family had I not been sent away.  And I begin to imagine what I would have been like if I had stayed.

During my last visit in 1992, my family was frustrated that we could not communicate better.  We managed to say things to each other through the use of a dictionary and bodily gestures.  My mother was anxious to describe why and how she gave me up.  I could not understand her, so I told her to tell it to my video camera.  I taped her story and tears, not fully understanding what she was saying.

Throughout my trip, my mother kept repeating one phrase which I did not understand at first.  By the end of the trip, it was loud and clear:  *"Marry a Korean man.  Have a baby, preferably a boy.  And come back to live in Korea."*

\* \* \*

This story is driven by a deep-seated desire to counter-document "truth" with my own statement of what is real, and to put into official existence a family story that is prone to forgetting.

# Completing My Puzzle...

## Wayne A. Berry (Oh, Ji Soo)

Being Korean and adopted has given me some unique perspectives on life--especially growing up in a small rural community in Isle, Minnesota (population 576), where fishing and wondering when the ice will thaw off the lake is the main talk of the town. Even though I always knew Korea was on the other side of the world from Minnesota, divided by a line I only knew as the DMZ, and my facial features and adoption papers told me I was Korean, for 22 years I wanted to be American like the people of Isle and all of my friends. American lifestyle was the only culture I knew, and I was comfortable with the surroundings I chose to be a part of. Korea to me was the place of the 1988 Olympics and the mother country of taekwondo. I had no memory of Korea (I was adopted when I was two years old), my birthfamily, the food, the culture--it was all erased once I became known as Wayne Alan Berry.

As a child, being called names like: *chink, Chinaman, rice paddy,* etc. and watching classmates pull up the corners of their eyes to mimic me only strengthened my actions to be as American as much as I could be. I was very careful not to display any signs of my Asian heritage. As comfortable as I pretended to be though, I could not deny the fact that I was Korean. I was always reminded of this when I looked in the mirror or paged through family photo albums, and saw my jet black hair in comparison to my mother and two sisters' red hair. But it took me 22 years to finally open the door, and explore a part of me that I so much didn't want anything to do with.

After I graduated from college and gradually met more Korean adoptees, I established a comfort level amongst these unfamiliar people and was surprised to find out there were others out there who came from similar backgrounds as I had. I thought I was the only Korean adoptee who grew up on a farm, played high school football and had a Caucasian girlfriend. I remember when I was first asked to be an instructor for a Korean culture camp in

Minnesota. I thought, "What did I have to offer these kids except that I, too, was adopted?" I knew absolutely nothing about Korea. Never did I think that this chain of events in such a short period of time would change my life forever.

Because of my curiosity and the fact that I had not been to Korea since 1972, I decided to make my first trip back during the summer of 1995. I also made up my mind that I was going to search for my birthfamily--something I had always thought about doing. After a lot of determination, letter writing and stubbornness, I was reunited with my Korean family during that same summer-- an emotional experience that I thought had very little chance of ever happening. During this process and my increased involvement with Korean adoption back in Minnesota, I felt an inner drive within me to share my experiences with other Korean adoptees and strengthen this community which had lacked a voice for so long. It also led me back to Korea for a nine-month stay in 1996-97, and to continue exploring a culture that is so foreign to me.

But Wayne, you are Korean--things should feel natural in Korea. You are in your mother country and with your Korean family. What's the problem? The problem is that I am very much a part of the country I was raised in, which is America. My mannerisms and language reflect American culture and I will never be viewed by the people of Korea as a "true" Korean.

So where is the happy medium to all of this? I am a minority in America because of my race, and I am also a minority in Korea because of my language. This challenge for me has been to find the peace, balance and acceptance of who I am, and to be proud of both my Korean and American heritage. As difficult as this is for me to understand at times, I know I am no less of an individual in the country I live in, nor in the country I was born in.

I am often asked if I am ever sad when I reflect back and think about all the realities that have happened to me growing up as a Korean adoptee. My answer to this question is that part of me is very sad, yet part of me is very thankful and appreciative of the life I was given by my American family. I think it's sad when a family is separated, regardless of whatever the reasons may be. I'm also sad to hear the testimonies of many Korean adoptees in the struggles they have had to endure in the search for their own identities. I'm sad I cannot speak to my Korean family openly, and express my true feelings to them without the use of a translator. As a result, I'm also sad that I will never fully understand my family, and vice versa, at the level of understanding the structure of a Korean family. But I have many blessings to be thankful for, and have always relied upon my faith in God to carry me through the difficult times, and to see the positives in the gift of life rather than the negatives. I have always been a firm believer that everything happens for a reason, and that everyone has potential to make a difference within the community they are involved in.

In conclusion, the past couple of years have marked a lot of changes in my life. As a result, I have compared it to completing a puzzle. Everyone in life has a puzzle to complete. For many Korean adoptees, they will live their entire life completely unaware of who they are as a Korean person, as I was doing for 22 years. Yet for others, they feel a burning passion to make connections with anything that has to do with Korea, and re-identify with a culture that was taken away from them at a very young age. We, as a Korean adopted community, will always have our adoption backgrounds as our commonality to each other. But we also have experiences that represent a special population in this world, and through these experiences we have become survivors. We need to strengthen each other and give the needed support that many of us have gone without for so many years...

# Now I'm Found

## Crystal Lee Hyun Joo Chappell

*Introduction:*
At the age of 4, Lee Hyun Joo was sent to America to be adopted.
Her name became Crystal Chappell. Like thousands of other
Korean adoptees, her birth family and culture were left behind.
Not until she was a young adult did she realize that something
was missing from her life. Going back to Korea she found out
what that was.

When I was two, I saw my father killed by a train. At least, it
seems likely that I did.

I'm told that I was there. I'm told I stood there by the tracks in
Kwangju, South Korea, on that scorching night in August 1976.

But I don't remember anything about that night: not the heat
soaking my clothes with sweat, not the cool wind that often called
my family to the wide open railroad corridor beside our house,
not the loud chatter of neighbors gathered at the tracks to drink
and socialize.

While my sister and I played, my father drank with his friends.
Tremendous stress from his work weighed him down. Slumped
over on the tracks, he was oblivious. He never heard his death
approaching.

I don't remember the roar of the train. I don't remember running
off the tracks to safety with the others. I don't remember my sister
crying in Korean, "Save my father!" But he couldn't be saved. He
was hurled headfirst onto an embankment and died hours later.

On that day, my name was Lee Hyun Joo. I was a Korean child in
a Korean family. The train came, and all that changed. My
father's death set off a chain of events that eventually sent me

halfway around the world to be adopted. Along with my older sister and younger brother, I became an American child in an American family. I lost all my memories of that life in Kwangju, that language, that land, and those parents.

Our journey mirrored ones taken by tens of thousands of Korean American adoptees every year since 1953, when Korean American adoption began in the aftermath of the Korean War. Since then, American families have adopted more than 110,000 Korean children. Korean children continue to come: about 1,400 more each year.

A generation of those adoptees is coming of age, and many are searching for answers about their adoption. Adoptee groups have formed, and organizations begun to help Korean adoptees find their birth families and celebrate their heritage.

Nearly 20 years after I left, I went back to Korea to meet my birth mother. In August 1996, I stood on those tracks and saw again where my birth father died, the spot where my journey to America began. In Korea, I found much more than I could have dreamed. I found the woman who gave birth to me. I found another family. I found pieces of memory. I found grief. I found love.

Now I know by heart the names of my birth mother--Kim Kwi Soon—and my birth father--Lee Sang Yul. The journey breathed new life into those names and my Korean one, giving me a new sense of peace I never knew I was missing.


*Blissful ignorance*

Growing up in the small town of Dimondale, Michigan, I didn't ask why I was adopted. All that mattered was that my parents, Garnet and Michael Chappell, loved us and that we were their children. My sister, younger brother and I were adopted together in 1978. She became Brooke and he became C.J. We joined Bromley, our older brother who also was a Korean American adoptee but not our blood relative.

Culture shock and the trauma of gaining a new family, home and identity erased my memory. In essence, I came to believe that I had been born on the day I was adopted, at age 4.

Still, as a child, I read our adoption papers and cried, unable to understand how our birth mother could have signed for our adoption. The sheets in my hands told little. They were the only proof I had of her existence.

For most of my life, I felt no interest in returning to Korea or finding my birth mother. In fact, I was proud of feeling that way. It seemed to prove that I loved my family and that I was "100 percent American."

Raised by white parents in a predominantly white town, I considered myself to be white. Others saw me differently, though. People stared at me as if I were an alien and children asked if I could see through my "Chinese, slant eyes."

The worst episodes were when teenage boys surrounded me on the school bus and yelled obscenities and racial slurs at me. My race shouldn't have mattered, I thought, because it didn't matter to my friends and family.

*Awakening and searching*

In college, new worlds of thought opened to me. Amid a boiling student struggle to create an Asian American Studies program at Northwestern University, I began to see myself as an Asian American and to see my race in positive ways.

That year, my sister and I decided to write to our birth mother.

For the first time since elementary school, I read our adoption papers again. My hand trembled. I covered my mouth to hold back tears rushing over me.

As I read the papers, I felt a hole growing inside me. The papers said that when I lived at a foster home in Seoul, I cried for my birth mother. It startled me to think that I had known who she was. That I had loved her and that being separated from her was painful. I couldn't imagine that. At 21, I didn't even know her name.

It astounded me that I had been able to suppress those memories and emotions so completely, that I had been able to forget my Korean heritage. I became more bothered that the whole first part of my life was nothing but blackness, a dark void in my mind.

Not knowing our birth mother's address or even if she was alive, we sent letters and pictures to her through our adoption agency, but officials there said it might take a year just to find her—if they could. Six months passed without a word. Like many adoptees who come up against similar walls, we soon found an alternative method.

*Miraculous connection*

That year, I began to seek out ways to connect with my Korean heritage, not knowing that it would open the door to my birth mother.

During a summer internship in Wichita, Kansas, I met the Rev. Suh Jung Kil at the Korean American Presbyterian Church. He was returning to Korea for the first time since he immigrated here in 1991.

Suh, who was as quick to laugh as he was to give of himself, offered to look for my birth mother. He took the only clues I had from the adoption papers: names, birth dates and places and death dates.

With help from his relatives, a police chief in Seoul, and an unknown, persistent telegram messenger, Suh found my birth mother in Yosu.

I was jumping, screaming and crying for joy after I heard the good news. I couldn't stop shaking for hours.

With a live connection to Korea, I started studying Korean language and began using my Korean name, Hyun Joo, among my Korean American friends. I hesitated to use the name of Lee, though, because I was unsure of the man it represented.

In the following months, my birth mother called without a translator just to hear our voices. I realized the hole she felt was three times as large as mine. I decided I had to go to Korea as soon as possible.

A year after Suh found my birth mother, my sister, younger brother and I took a 12-hour flight to South Korea, not knowing what we would find in the Land of the Morning Calm.

### Reunited at last

At Kimpo Airport in Seoul, I pushed the luggage cart forward and lifted my meager notepaper sign showing our Korean names. We were surrounded by Korean faces, looking at my sister, younger brother and me hopefully, then disappointedly as they realized we weren't who they were looking for. I couldn't bare to look. Our birth mother could appear at any second.

No one responded. Disappointed, I stopped and looked back at Brooke and C.J. We had been delayed two hours in immigrations and customs lines. Maybe we were too late.

Then someone yelled our Korean names, "Hyun Joo! Joo Mee! Jong Suk!" I looked toward the voice. Pushing her way to the front of the crowd, an agile woman, wearing a vibrant pink shirt and flowing black pants, waved eagerly. I recognized my birth mother instantly, seeing her resemblance to her photos and feeling odd, as if I was looking at myself.

I ran toward her. I ran so fast that my cart hit the dividing rail in front of her. My birth mother and I stood face to face. She smiled lovingly, then motioned excitedly to go to the left, to the opening of the rail. We both ran in that direction, hurrying through the crowd.

Falling into each other's arms, we began to cry. She wailed; her cries mourned a separation that no parent wants to endure. My heart ached as a deep pain released through my tears.

Of all the Korean phrases I had learned, I managed to say only, "Gwen-chan-ah-yo," meaning "Don't worry. It's OK." I was finally back, in my birth mother's arms, in my country of birth.

Soon, we were surrounded by our unknown relatives: my Korean stepfather, uncles, cousins, distant cousins and their friends and families. They gazed at us with wide eyes, amazed to see that 7-year-old Joo Mee had turned 25, that 4-year-old Hyun Joo was 22, and that baby Jong Suk was 19.

They hugged us and cried in relief, expressing overwhelming emotion in Korean that I didn't understand. It moved me. I hadn't imagined that our return would affect so many others so deeply.

Then I crumbled before my 83-year-old grandmother—hunched over at half my size and I'm 5-foot-1. She was the grandmother I had never known; in her I saw the embodiment of my Korean heritage standing before me.

## A mirror of myself

A seven-hour train ride took us from Seoul to the southern port city of Yosu. My birth mother sat next to me, and, looking at my hands, she laughed in surprise.

She lifted mine next to hers and playfully slapped it. Our hands were identical; hers were only more wrinkled.

We share a physical bond I could never imagine before. In the next two weeks, we would be continually amazed that we had the same feet, arms, knees, personality traits. Even a personal tic was mirror perfect: We both have the habit of scrunching our eyes tightly and repeatedly from time to time.

I delighted in being part of her flurry of activity from daybreak to midnight. At 50, she runs a savings credit circle that she began among friends, does all the housework and attends Presbyterian church almost every day.

As we developed a strong bond, we created our own language, mixing Korean and English and using nods, grunts and facial expressions that amused my sister.

*Long-awaited answers*

On the second day in Korea, we learned about pieces of our past that only my birth mother could know.

My birth mother lives with my stepfather, Chi Chong Rae, and two half-brothers, Min Gook and Jung Gook, on a close-knit street. Girls ride bikes and boys play pogs as they scream, "Kaowi! Paowi! Bo!" (Scissors! Rock! Paper!)

The lunchtime smells of *bulgogi* (marinated beef), spicy *kimchi* and seafood stews lingered in the air.

Inside my birth mother's shady house, we returned to a darker time. Sitting in a circle on the floor of Min Gook's room, we listened intently as Susan, a Korean Canadian friend from my birth mother's church, translated difficult questions and answers.

I knew that this was painful for my birth mother; remembering the past seemed to settle a physical weight onto her shoulders, which slumped. The night of my birth father's death replayed in her mind as she described what the adoption papers couldn't: why.

With the help of the translator, she told this story. When my birth father died, she was eight months pregnant with my younger brother, C.J. Because he died in a train accident without insurance, my birth mother had to pay for everything, including fees to

130

the rail company for any damage to the train.

Korea's recession compounded her desperation. Our extended family helped as much as they could, but they had no rice fields or assets.

On top of our poverty, her grief was unimaginable. She had loved Lee Sang Yul since she was 16 and had dated him for nine years before they married.

Alone, she hated hearing the train by our house. The powerful rumbling was an unbearable reminder. It drove her to move to a new home, where C.J. was born. She took us everywhere, even to work.

She tried to support us by selling insurance, books and other things. She tried for almost three years to raise us on her own, she said, and her expression showed how determined she'd been.

But like tens of thousands of single mothers in Korea's patrilineal society and poverty of the 1970s, she found it impossible and turned to U.S. adoption.

"She thought she was sending you guys to America, not losing you, but sending you to school," said Susan, the translator.

*Regrets of a lifetime*

At this point in the story, our birth mother paused. Tears came to her eyes, and she bit her thumb to control her sobbing. I crossed the room and put my arm around her shoulders. Her voice quivered as Korean phrases spilled from her lips. Susan, who is a young mother, also began crying.

My birth mother said that after we went to America, she wanted to kill herself.

For the first time, I heard my younger brother weep. He wrapped his arms around my birth mother and me, and we all cried.

131

My birth mother said she couldn't eat and couldn't be alone. Whenever she saw children crying, she would go to them and cry. She worried that one of us was dead and prayed for us every day.

Her friends, including our future stepfather, persuaded her to stay alive by saying, "If they grow up and want to see you, they will have no one. No mother. No father."

I cried harder, knowing that my birth mother had stayed alive for us, for this time when we would return. Tremendous guilt came over me because I had denied her for so long.


*Meeting my birth father*

That outpouring of memory and grief strengthened our connection to our birth mother, and answered questions that had lingered over our whole lives. Our relationship deepened a few days later when we visited an uncle and aunt in a remote village, about two hours northwest of Yosu.

There, two memories of childhood returned to me: They were only a steep path and a cracked wall. But nonetheless, they were places I remembered--tangible connections to my past.

My birth father was buried near his brother's home. We visited his burial mound, and cried there during a ceremony.

Walking away from the grave, I paused to soak in my birth father's surroundings and was pleased. His body rests in green flowing rice fields surrounded by shadowy mountains and a vast blue sky.

Alone on the path, I cried for my lost father for whom I had never grieved. I had traveled thousands of miles to find my Korean heritage. But I had to acknowledge that I couldn't find the man whose blood runs through my veins.

I wanted so badly to know him as I knew my birth mother. And I called out "father" in Korean, "Appah ..."

As if in response, my uncle appeared just past the large branch in front of me. He came to check on me. He took my hand and walked with me as I stopped sobbing. Though our palms were soaked with sweat from the glaring sun, I was happy to hold his.

A familiar feeling came over me and I pictured myself as a little girl walking down this trail while holding my birth father's hand. I felt as if my uncle was acting in my birth father's role. His pleased smile showed that he felt good fulfilling the duty to his brother.

Soon I would see the home that we shared with our birth father.

*Where it started*

On an overcast day, we traveled four hours from Yosu to the city of my childhood, Kwangju, the bustling capital of the Southwestern province and the site of the Kwangju Uprising for democracy on May 18, 1980, which ended in a bloody massacre by government troops.

South Korean flags flew from every flagpole on streets crowded with bright Korean signs. Surrounded by Koreans from every walk of life, we returned with our birth mother to our old neighborhood.

The dilapidated housing nearby made my heart sink. We stood in front of our old house. A sad silence fell upon us. We examined the small, cluttered courtyard of the five connected one-story houses. I couldn't remember anything, but a familiar and unsettling feeling was creeping over me.

My birth mother pointed to the tracks; they were behind a high wall, and within seconds, a train roared by--only a few feet away. It filled me with horror to stand that close to the ferocious rumbling.

We went to the tracks and stood at the rocky, unmarked rail crossing sandwiched between two walls of crowded housing. My birth father's accident happened only steps away from our old gate.

No one was in sight. It was silent and eerie. The last time I stood in this place was the night he was killed.

At first glance, I guessed the spot where he was hit. I don't know if that was memory or intuition. Soon, my birth mother sat on the tracks, showing us how he was killed. Earlier she had told us that he was exhausted by his work as a laborer at city hall. Under a lot of stress, he drank heavily. Sitting slumped over on the tracks, he was oblivious to the train.

I was amazed by her strength.

The way she moved—stiffly, without any of her characteristic grace or energy—signaled that she was bracing herself for grief. Still, she spoke clearly, repeating key phrases and acting out motions to make sure I understood, so that I could translate for Brooke and C.J.

A few minutes later, I came back to the tracks alone. I wished my birth father were alive. If he hadn't been killed, I most likely wouldn't have been sent on this lifelong odyssey to learn about what had been. To lose my birth mother and find her again. To learn about what it meant to be Korean.

At the same time, I thought that if he hadn't died, I never would've known my American family and friends, or any of my life here. I felt a sense of resolution having come full circle, standing where it all began. The discovery makes a whole part of my past a vital part of my future.

I couldn't help wondering, though, who I would be if he were alive. The drizzling rain thickened into cold drops. The sky seemed to be crying, and I returned to my birth mother.

*Embracing names*

When I returned to Minneapolis, so many faces, places and feelings filled my mind, but a few things were clear. I loved my Korean mother as much as I loved my American parents. And I knew I could take the name of Lee. Now I have two complete names: one Korean, one English. They encompass my two worlds, two families and two identities that sometimes clash, sometimes combine and sometimes coexist.

One quiet night at my birth mother's house, our stepfather carefully wrote our Korean names and their meanings. Lee represents a tree seedling. Hyun Joo means beautiful bright light, which is surprisingly close to my American name of Crystal.

He pointed to the words and told us to treasure them. I didn't know how to tell him that I already did.

*Afterword:*

Months after personally processing our trip to Korea and finding more answers, I often remember a moment that keeps resounding in my life.

We were wiping away tears after our birth mother told us how her friends helped her stay alive. My sister, who usually shunned references to God, surprisingly gave one of her own. With assurance and wonder, she happily said, "So that shows how God really worked in our lives."

Susan, the translator, agreed, smiling and adding, "And it was lucky that you three stayed together in the same house."

The miracles have been countless: that God kept us alive after our birth father's death, adopted us into such a loving family, reunited us with our birth mother, and filled the reunion with love and healing.

I remain in awe of God's power and faithfulness. And I'm thankful for continued blessings as we build our Korean American family and as the adoptee community grows as a family.

*Seeds of Resolution*

# Generation Me

## Rebekah Jin Turner

I am my own generation.
I'm not first, second, or even third;
like so many of you.
I am Generation Me.
I journeyed alone long ago;
from the Land of the Morning Calm.
Over the water, in a plane, on a lap,
to fulfill someone else's dream
of having a family.
Destination:
the House of Insanity.
Spineless father, Psychotic mother, Ghost brother.
Hell. Secrets. Nightmares.
Now I am leaving.  Where?  To a place
Over the water, in a plane, in peace...

# Save A Place For Me

## Mi Ok Song Bruining

*To the Spirit of Peter Young Sip Kim*

One night, in the chilly stillness
of silence, I dreamed
a dream where I fell asleep
and never woke up.
I heard your voice, calling my name,
in a gentle, breathless whisper.

I felt your presence and you appeared
before me--younger
than when you were alive
and seeming a bit smaller--
older than a child, but more innocent
than when I knew you.

"Anne," you said--for you knew me
by my adopted name,
"My suicide was painless--just as the theme song
to the M.A.S.H. t.v. show said.
It didn't hurt when I felt my last breath
slipping away."

I felt the disturbing, familiar sense of comfort
by your words and pleaded to you,
"It didn't have to end this way, Peter."
In an attempt to relieve my guilt and remorse,
I said, "I tried, but failed to help you."
"Yes, Anne, you did try," you reassured me.
"But, Anne, it is not accidental
that I died exactly one month before
my alleged thirty-first birthday."

"I know," I said, understanding

140

that you never made it back to Korea,
as you had dreamed of,
and you never felt the soil of your birth land
under your feet--as I did.

We talked of suicide often,
of your two previous attempts--
when you were alive and still of this earth.
It was never a morbid topic for us--
but a secret desire and seductive fear
we shared as kindred spirits.

When I tell my friends of your death,
Peter, of your profound loss--
they ask: Why? Did you and I know?
Because, I reason: it was about being adopted
and feelings--of being different,
never belonging, never feeling whole
nor complete, feeling rejected and discarded
and yes, you and I know.

I still know why and I still know
of your pain, your struggle, your loss
and despair, because I also
dance with the idea of ending the pain,
but cannot bring myself to end my life.

I tell my remaining friends
of your suicide, Peter,
because your sadness and regrets
and trauma and rage must not be forgotten.
Your gentle spirit continues to live
and your humor remains
in me as a testament to your strength
and resilience that is a gift
of your friendship
and former relationship to me.

The anguish and agony you leave behind
in the wake of your suicide

is the tragedy for those who knew you, Peter.
I still berate myself with "what ifs?"
but believe that your death was the only way
for you to attain peace and tranquility.

"Yes, Anne," you said. "I don't feel anything
anymore. It is a kind of peace
I didn't have when I was alive."
I looked at you and you said,
"I must go now, Anne."
"Okay, Peter," I said reluctantly,
"Will you save a place for me,
next to you?" I asked.

You smiled and said, "Yes, Anne,
but don't come soon."
Then, you disappeared into the darkness.
I closed my eyes, and felt the warmth
of a flickering flame--so close,
I could touch it.

# Dear Luuk

## Kari Ruth

Dear Luuk,

As a writer, I usually am not at a loss for written words--but I struggle now to find a way to reach you.

My night's dark calm has been disturbed by troubling thoughts since your death. The light of my days has revealed unsettling conclusions.

Driving home in the throngs of rush-hour gridlock on the day I received news of your death, I could only think of your pain through my tears. I never thought to wonder, "Why?" I only wished I could have carried the weight of your anguish for you.

I may never understand why you ended your life, Luuk, but I do understand your need to find peace.

Being adopted Korean is far more complex than choosing racial designation. You knew that.

The struggles of racial identity cannot be solved at culture camps, outreach events, panel discussions or trips to our birth country. They cannot be described as growing pains nor diagnosed with color-blind love. We both discovered that for ourselves.

Our search for ourselves does not have an end--neither does the pain. You saw that, but you couldn't see a way to ease the difficulty of your earthly journey. Somewhere along the way, you forgot to open your eyes and catch a glimpse of hope.

A friend recently commented that we, as adopted Koreans, live a lie. In order to assimilate into not only a white society, but also our own adoptive families, we learn to see ourselves as others want to see us. We turn our lies into betrayal--of ourselves.

143

Maybe you got tired of wearing your mask. Maybe you forgot who existed beneath the weight of that facade.

You and I, Luuk, have traveled so far--and for what?

I have heard parents commenting that adopting Korean children is an enriching cultural experience and that other adults should do the same.

Those parents must not understand that the price they paid for us was insignificant compared to the price we pay to fit into their world.

Society has already told you and me that we have become Americans because of someone else's charity. Now we're being told that our cultural displacement had a purpose--multiculturalism. By growing up in white families, we can be examples, Luuk. We can show others that racial harmony is possible. We just can't show our burdened backs.

We allay our parents' fears by internalizing our own.

I guess someone forgot to ask us if we wanted to be America's diversity mascots.

Luuk, I think about you every day. I am reminded of you when I look in the mirror. I see the reflection of your morality in my eyes and the eyes of other adopted children and adults.

And I still see a flicker of hope.

Maybe there is a reason for all of this, but I refuse to turn your suicide into a martyr's message. You sacrificed too much of yourself in life; I won't take away what is left of you in death.

I hope you have found your peace, friend.

   *Kari.*

# My Story...Thus Far
## Remembering the Abuse, Healing the Pain

### Su Niles

I am a Korean born adoptee, age 38, living a modest life in California. One would think that says it all. It does not. Reverting to the adage, "You can't tell a book by its cover," I do not, fortunately, wear my life experiences on my face. Good thing.

I was born in 1959, somewhere in Korea, and left on the steps of City Hall in Seoul. That's what it says in the two-paper file that resides at the orphanage where I was transferred. No note, no name, no real birth date. Like so many of us, I simply appeared. Two months later, I was in America, nearly dead, adopted by a white couple.

Lucky me. I was raised on my mother's heroic effort to keep me alive after the flight, spoon-fed "You're so lucky" lines and dressed up like—you guessed it—a China doll. I guess they got confused. And I hate the word "lucky".

There I was, along with my sister who is also Korean-born, in a home where everything was about Kansas, the Depression, gratitude and lines drawn around us by the looks on our faces. And I was trapped by my mother. A mother whose love, I believe, became confused with manipulation and demanded blind devotion. A mother who said, "I love you," while she back-handed me; a mother who told me that I was lucky that my [birth] mother didn't leave me in the streets to die like the other prostitutes did; a mother, who in her twisted sense of what love was, violated my body in a ritualistic, sadistic manner. My friends call it torture. So do I.

I'd like to say alcoholism precipitated all of this, but while both of my adoptive parents were champion alcoholics, my mother's disease didn't come to the fore until my high school years. My father, by virtue of his alcoholism, was guilty of neglect. He, however, never laid a hand on me. How ironic.

Then there were the fears. I was a child of fear. My first recollection of panic attacks was at the age of 6. They have been my companion all through my childhood and into adulthood. Twice in my life, thus far, panic has debilitated me to the point that I could not function. There were times I wished I would simply die. There were times I tried to make it happen. I'm still here.

In between the panic attacks, I managed to get a job, hold onto it and excel at it. By the time I reached 27, after five grueling years of in-home care, my mother finally died — strokes, complicated by alcoholism. I thought it would resolve the complex feelings I had. It only exacerbated them. What's new?

So, I decided to work very hard at dealing with them, put them behind me and go forward. One issue would be laid to rest and another would pop up its ugly head to replace it. It was so kindly put to me by my therapist that it took 26 years to damage the physical and emotional me, how could I expect it to be fixed so quickly? Like all good medicine, it was tough to take.

Much of what I know now I had to remember. Or rather, it came to me through memories. I had pushed it all away. Little by little, it came seeping back. The put-downs, the verbal abuse, they came first. Like watching a movie inside my head, it was all there in panoramic technicolor. I felt its authenticity in my gut. I wondered if all adoptive parents of Korean born children treated them like me. In the process of healing these wounds, I found a new, strange part of me. The Korean part.

I don't think anyone knows what's missing in life until someone comes along and opens a window. That someone for me was a first generation Korean psychiatrist, Dr. Luke I. C. Kim. He shared with me, among other people, his story of being in the North before the Korean War and how his family struggled to get to the South. It is a moving, pain-filled story, and I felt immediately akin to him. Thus began my journey into discovering in my soul what I wear on my face: Being Korean.

146

Dr. Kim, his wife Grace, and consequently many of his friends accepted me—despite being taught all my life that Koreans hated me—and educated me on Korean ethos, language, food, everything. Everything they could give me, they did. And still do.

I realized that I come from a very strong people. The Korean Americans I knew had endured hardships that I judged to be much worse than mine, yet they triumphed. The only difference was they all had strong family structures to nurture each other against the harsher outside world. Growing up, I had no such haven because the enemy lived within the house. But their strength, I realized, was mine too. I embraced this realization and was glad of it, because the greatest test so far was to come.

On a lazy Saturday morning last August, nearing the end of the month, my husband and I were talking casually about this and that. In the middle of some innocuous conversation, he said a single word, and I was galvanized. Like some sonic tidal wave, pictures, smells, sounds, tastes came flooding into me in a sensory overload. It was the most recent of my flashbacks to my childhood, the most humiliating part: My mother's violation of my body.

I remembered everything. The stench. The crying. Her watching me. The cold, cold water. Years before, I remember my brother saying I used to scream in the bathroom. I couldn't recollect it then. But now, during this memory onslaught, everything fell into place and made complete sense: His remark, why my body doesn't function properly, why I panic in the night. I had been diagnosed with Post Traumatic Stress Disorder on three separate occasions, but we could never pinpoint the trauma. It was now pinpointed.

So, I tried to handle it. Pragmatically at first, then philosophically. But this one cut me deeply. I wasn't rebounding. After several months, I fell into a deep depression. Depressions for me came and went, alternating with agitating highs where I could trash the house in a matter of seconds in a blinding rage. Not pretty behavior. Not fun to live with.

147

I was referred to another psychiatrist for the depression. I talked. He listened. He was compassionate. Calm. I wanted to die. Didn't shed a tear. Told him everything I could think of. He caught something in what I said. "Agitation." He asked questions. He asked more. And he diagnosed me with what I felt was one more blow to this already established freak show of a life: Bi-Polar or Manic-Depressive Illness. I do not think I hated my mother any more than was humanly possible. It was a very good thing she was already dead. A very good thing indeed.

### Today

In Al-Anon, a support group for family and friends of alcoholics, I learned 13 years ago that I must "live life one day at a time." It's all I get. Some things I have no choice but to deal with everyday. I take medication for the Bi-Polar and the panic attacks. There is no choice, unless I want to live in emotional hell. But I have things to do, stories to tell, and a kind of wacky mission which cannot be accomplished unless I take care of myself. I'll be damned if the pain I've experienced isn't put to good use. I'm determined to make sure that I put it to good use. Too many people are senselessly hurt at the hands of others—I don't have a special lock on pain—and if sharing this brings something positive to someone, especially a Korean adoptee, a stranger living in her own land, then my life will not have been wasted. If someone has walked down the same trail of tears, then my pain will not have been for nothing. And as for my mother...well, she certainly didn't accomplish what she wanted. Almost. But not quite.

# Mommy Dearest*

## Mihee-Nathalie Lemoine

Mommy Dearest,

I want to tell you that I have thought about you a great deal, you
and your country.

I want to tell you that here in Belgium, you are not well known.
Your country is the land of the morning calm,
the country divided along the 38th parallel,
for the SPCA, is the land of the dog eaters
Oh scandal, our reputation has been tarnished,
to be re-established only after the Olympic games.

I want to tell you that I don't regret having left.
That I was one of the lucky ones--
that luck was what you hoped for me?

I want to tell you that I have been affected by Belgian apathy
that my Koreanness smells like fried potatoes,
my Belgianness like kimchi.

I want to tell you that living among your people has given me a
different view of things...
The Korean passion for alcohol astonished me.
If I accept my Koreanness, it is only by default.
I cannot see Koreans as they really are, only as they wish to be
seen.

I want to make you see that there is strength in the Koreanness
of one who has been raised in Korea.
But if one is only Korean on the outside, what is our identity,
except that coming from a nation that survived the cruel
Japanese occupation,
a nation that gave away its surplus of orphans.

I want to tell you that after dreaming, blaming, envying, and finally living in your land, this short time can in no way make up the years of exile.

Finally, I want to tell you that I will depart from here as I came, but not by your side, Mommy dearest, especially not by your side.

*The title comes from the book entitled, "Mommy Dearest" written by an adopted daughter of the actress Joan Crawford. The adoptee endured an abusive life with the actress, and this book tells her story.*

*Translated from French, this text is the narrative of my film (short) in Super 8, made in 1988.*

*To my genitors, to my parents,*
*Mihee-Nathalie Lemoine*

# On Being Adopted

## *Kim Maher*

Little one, who cries for you?
Your mother and father care
Who is my mother?
Who is my father?
The womb that held me?
Or the arms that hold me?
The man that made me?
Or the heart that molds me?
Both, my child, both
The ones who gave you life
And the ones who give you life
The ones who bore you
And the ones who adore you
Don't shame either
For both are your creators

# Obstacles and Challenges

## Su Niles

I am struggling. Alternately strong and excited, then sad and angry, I am working my way through some sort of life maze. If this reads as though I am going in a multitude of directions, then it is an accurate reflection of what's happening inside of me.

My journey is two-fold: To lay to rest the past and create for myself a future. Sometimes I want to just give up, but then, I see the prize before me, and continue on.

This has been my most difficult challenge: To overcome the effects of a turbulent childhood. My adoptive parents were alcoholics, my mother emotionally and physically abusive to me, and because I was Korean in an all-white family, I fought the feelings of isolation and loneliness. Other adoptees have similar stories to share: the degenerative effects of alcoholism, the humiliation of sexual abuse, the eating away of your self-esteem when your adoption gets continually thrown in your face.

There are many of us out there, working through these very real obstacles. We are, collectively, functional, bright and articulate. We utilize these things to hide our feelings of shame, inadequacy and deep, deep hurt. I used to downplay my experiences. No longer. If indeed the truth shall set us free, then I must adhere to that belief in my personal life. What I experienced was real, painful and perhaps, even beyond complete repair. I continue to find a way to work through these issues so I can put them away. I do this for my future, and how I want to live.

The future frightens me, yet I am intrigued. Carrying the scars only makes my challenge greater. And that challenge is to find my place within the Korean community. Having no contact with anything Korean as a child and young adult, I am determined to make up for lost years. It is an exciting, fulfilling, yet sad journey, too. Culturally, I am an American. Raised on steak, potatoes,

McDonald's and fried chicken, this hardly prepared me for *bulgo - gi, mandu, kimchee* or *chapchae*.

This is just the basic level. There is an emotional tie that is indescribable. I am compelled to assimilate all that I can about Korea and what being Korean means. At the same time, I recognize all too deeply some inescapable facts. Regardless of how many Korean cultural events I attend, regardless of how much of the Korean language I learn, and regardless of how many Korean friends I make, I will never, ever regain in full measure what I have lost. This is my greatest sorrow. Once my birthmother relinquished me and I was flown to America, all those ties to Korea were cut. I will never be wholly Korean.

I walk in this skin. And in this skin, I am any American. A single image has been etched inside of me. American pie, From Sea to Shining Sea... all semantics. But my skin conflicts with me. The world sees me as a Color. Crossing the culture gap with other pioneers who are braving the elements of their own prejudices, I realize how much energy it takes to open the mind, however willing the spirit. And I slam up against the impenetrable wall.

It hurts so much to be on the outside. It is altogether a lovely pain, one with which I am intimate. This skin has cost me dearly. My elementary school phrases are a flag that denotes my infancy in this world I am visiting. *Ahnyong hasayo, kamsa hamnida...* conversational Korean. But my skin conflicts with me once again. Listening to the melody of this language spoken by its natives in the comfort of their conference, I realize how far I have to go, despite how far I've come. And I press myself against the impenetrable wall.

I walk in this skin. And in this skin, I have found another world. Not in America, not in Korea... but where? I cannot wholly accept one and wholly reject the other. It is painful, to embrace two worlds, to tie the laces of the insides of me. Closely resembling a war within where there is neither victor nor vanquished, I understand--perhaps too late--this may well be my destiny. To sit forever by the impenetrable wall.

So, I must take what I can. Through the years of understanding the impact of intercountry adoption on myself and other adoptees, I have finally come to accept these things: I am Korean. I will always be Korean. I can no more alter that than I can my gender. And I am going forward to the goal I've set before me: To attain the best of my ability the culture that, by birth, truly belongs to me.

# Lying On My Back

## Eun Jung Che

my hand wanders over the contours of my body
and rests over the soft arch of my belly
the subtle swell that represents the hollow of promise
       one day, we will fill it with the continuation of us
i wonder what those moments will mean
as my stomach rises and reaches away from the small of my back
what will this mean, when i begin to unravel myself
       in preparation to reknit the fabric with the thread of a
       new life

i think of the history that has sunk deep into these bones
the legacy that i have inherited
       how unwelcome the pain and the silence
the two elements feeding upon each other
       growing with time
i think of how this legacy has exiled me to the far reaches of this
earth
the weight of my loyalties press down on me
the way i was told to endure
anger as deep and as old as the waves that separate me
       from my homeland

can i take my infant daughter
and cradle her in my arms
and tell her that she is safe
will i begin to even think or hope that lie to be true
i pray my womb will someday be filled
but the joy is not justified
for it will be me who will allow this cycle to continue
it will be me who provides yet another young child
       to be eaten and torn by the country born on her blood

my fear is that she will be pretty, or very, very smart
or that her spirit will be fearless and unperturbable

for mediocrity is the only road for safety
        demise her only true shelter
i begin to understand that silence that follows my people
like a cloud that circled the earth

for if she is a beacon of light
her fire will only illuminate the rest of us
destroying the darkness our parents have tried to cloak us in
        we've seen our own bones
as i step toward light, i fear i am only creating smoke
that will choke and suffocate
        the generations from which i came
        and those that will come from me

such weight lies below my hand
such roots

how do i tell her of what i've seen
of what they will try to do to her
and keep her hoping

rage sweeps over all of us
leaving no cradle of the american *gaijin*
        unrocked

do i dare hope
that her eyes will be

        like mine?


        *gaijin--*"foreigner" in Japanese


156

# To You Korea, Mother Nation

### Mihee-Nathalie Lemoine

I would ask you to look at us
We, the adoptees of Korea
Not with pity
We, adopted overseas

I will ask you
Not to forget that
We have the *han* flowing through our veins
We have the same face as yours
We have hearts though sometimes in pain
Despite us, we have your genes

I would insist
Not to forget that
Even if we see the same moon
Despite the differences, we are bound

I would like
Not to forget
Even for Songsu Bridge and
Sampoong in the news
Despite the distance, we are bound

At a time when Korea is globalizing
Or rather wants to open up to the world
At a time when Korea spends
to glorify its name
At a time when Korea loses itself
in its social problems

We, the adoptees of Korea
we ask you
We adoptees, Koreans from the outside,
To no longer deny.

--Seoul 1993

# *Never*

## *Ellwyn Kauffman*

I never asked to be born to those who wouldn't have me
I never asked to be left in Sajik Park for fate
I never asked to become the son of a white couple.
None of this was mine to ask.
I never had a chance to learn your language
or your customs
wear the Hanbok,
pour and receive properly.
Rice was rarely eaten in my home
I grew up on bedtime stories and powdered milk,
hot dogs and Mother Goose,
chewable vitamins and violin lessons.

I never asked to be stared at
called a gook and a chink.
taught never to fight back
have the courage not to hear.
Courage or cowardice?
I swallowed my bile
choked as it went down
just words
from people who knew better
but spit them at me anyway.
God loves you and them
everyone.
Nothing else matters.
Burn in Hell, I still thought.

I never knew why I cried when my parents
were gone for too long
never trusted myself
always mimicked, copied, plagiarized,
nice to a fault, willing to sacrifice too much
tried to be all things to everyone.
They must accept me

dutiful son, foreign-faced kid
endear, curry favor, follow
be, do, talk like them
plow their fertile lives
instead of the one I was handed
become a futile, ardent shadow.


An ache, a yearning emptiness
in the pit of me
Korea should be there
the food, the language, the legacy.
I miss this now
Most of all
I miss my own past.


I never knew who gave birth to me,
which streets or shores, hills or flats
I came from
cousins, aunts, uncles
if my birth family is still there
I am an odd mark
a dark footnote.
If those who brought me into life
want nothing to do with me
I will accept it
only after I know this —
why I was left in a park
on the Fourth of July
as sure as the sun
I have a right to know
of that independence day.


I never want to hear that my past should be left alone
that what I'm searching for are ghosts.
Would I be here if my past wasn't real?
Don't think I don't belong here in Korea
Korea is mine as it is yours
I may not know how to speak to you
I may not know anything of this place
but tell me not to worry

tell me I'm a fool to want to find anything
tell me you know what I've been through
and I will ball my words up in a fist
shouting in your face—
y ɔu will never know me
you will never understand
you will never know my life

Tell me to go away
tell me my problems are too deep to be touched
and I will reach down and find
my years of pretending to be deaf
the horrible results of good intentions
fueled with ignorance.
I will show you anger
my rage with no place to go
all in a seething torrent
if you dismiss me
if you exclude me
if you tell me what it is to be Korean
and leave me no room.

# *jap*

## *Lee Herrick*

windshield to windshield
we are parked
like matadors,
pumping gas at the am pm.
It is a normal afternoon in the valley
like all afternoons in the valley,
split between modern duty
and the desire of something better.

We are in the same world.
I pull in and
face you, but
my sunglasses shield my almond
eyes, and what you don't realize
is that I see you.
I see you
in your red anger,
your believed anonymity
your life boiling you to this ugly place,
where, in the pain of inarticulacy,
your vomit words,
like swords,
hurled at me:

*god      damn      jap*

I look down at my chest
my almond eyes open wide
breath sputtering
blood dripping.
I pull it from just beside my heart
and I still stand.

This is where racism begins

in the throat
at the station
in the heart of valley afternoons.

I hold your bloody words,
walking to you slowly
with sword in hand.
I have been here before, have you?
I can show you knife wounds
on my chest
like constellations

I approach you and you fear
something, my difference
I imagine
Instead of thrusting this bloody sword
back into you and killing us both off
slowly, I whisper to you:

*I am not god*
*I am not damned*
*and I am not Japanese*

I drop the sword and feel
my chest, stronger
and I imagine a space
with no swords
and
no constellations

# *yellow*

## *Nabiya*

**yellow**
known as
a color that breeds anxiety.
not black, not white.
**yellow**
also the color
of the sun's rays.
**yellow**
a symbol
of brightness and warmth,
both essential to survival.
**yellow**
also the color
of tropical bananas.
**yellow**
a symbol
of protective peels
preserving an inner sweet.
**yellow**
also the color
of oval shaped lemons.
**yellow**
a symbol
of clean refreshment,
though bitter when bitten.
**yellow**
also the color
of a people no longer silent.
**yellow**
a symbol
of potential revolution.
not black, not white.
**yellow**
**no wonder we make you anxious.**

163

# Full Circle

## *Nabiya*

As I embarked on my quest
To the mecca of my soul,
A wise man told me:
"Worry + worry = worry"
In words I did not yet understand.
My mind could only envision people--
Families full of secrets,
Faces full of repression,
Pasts full of shame--
Whose lives were branded by child
Who brought disgrace
Just by being;
A family haunted by a living ghost
Culture forced them to deny;
A mother and child dictated
Fates of anonymity
To save an honor more sacred
Than the pangs of guilt and desire;
A newborn victim,
Lost somewhere in the shadows
Of the unchangeable.

In the land of my mother,
I turn twenty.
With the death of my adolescence
The wise man's warning burns into my heart
And forever locks me out of the world
Which existed in my little girl dreams.
A final realization that both
The beginning and the end
Eternally hide within the depths
Of the unknown;
And the circle is complete.

# Contributors' Notes

## Me-K. Ahn

Much of Me-K. Ahn's work focuses on her experience as an adopted Korean woman. In addition to filmmaking, she uses writing as a way to reconstruct unknown histories. She has received numerous grants for filmmaking and writing, including a 1995 Jerome Foundation Film/Video Grant and a 1994-5 Loft-McKnight Award in Creative Prose. Her fiction and essays have been published in *COLORS Magazine, dIS\*orient Journalzine, Loft-McKnight Award Anthology* and *The Adoption Reader*, an adoption anthology published by Seal Press.

## Grant Barnes

Grant Barnes is an adoptee who grew up in Texas, where he studied philosophy and comparative literature, spent three years in Europe during and after college, and did graduate work in international relations and law at Harvard. Although Grant is a practicing attorney who works closely with German and Swedish corporate clients, he is licensed in Hawaii, as well as New York and California. He has been writing poetry since childhood and keeps returning to Donne, Milton, Melville, Stevens as well as Hawaiian sources for challenge and inspiration. Grant currently lives in the Koreatown area of Los Angeles.

## Wayne Berry (Oh Ji Soo)

I am 27 years old and a school teacher in Eagan, Minnesota which is a suburb of the Minneapolis/St. Paul area. I was adopted when I was two years old into a small, rural community in central Minnesota with a population of 575 people. I have been back to Korea twice since my adoption. The first time was in 1995. During this trip, I spent 12 days traveling the country and I also met my birthfamily for the first time in 24 years. My second trip was a nine-month stay from September 1996 to May 1997. This was a very fulfilling and educational trip for me because I had a chance to get to know my Korean family better, and I also gained a greater appreciation of the Korean culture.

I am very active in the Korean adopted community in Minnesota by being a member of MAK (Minnesota Adopted Koreans), and an instructor at a number of the Korean adoptee camps in and around the state. In 1996, I established the Korean Adoption Registry to assist other Korean adoptees in the search for their own biological family.

### Deann Borshay

Deann Borshay served as Executive Director of NAATA (National Asian American Telecommunications Association) from 1993 to 1996. She has represented Asian American communities within the Minority Public Broadcasting Consortia, testified on behalf of minority independent producers before the U.S. Congress during authorization hearings, and served as an active member of national coalitions tracking policy development in public broadcasting, arts funding, and new technologies. She has consulted on local and national public television projects and served as co-executive producer for the award-winning documentary, A.K.A. DON BONUS by Spencer Nakasako. She is currently directing and producing the documentary, *Remembering the Way Home*. Ms. Borshay is a graduate of U.C. Berkeley and holds a Master's Degree in Psychology.

### Kimberly J. Brown

Kimberly J. Brown, age 25, was born in Korea, adopted at 17 months and grew up in a suburb of Minneapolis where she currently lives. Three of her poems were published recently by the National Library of Poetry. She works at a financial printing company in St. Paul, MN and will receive a Bachelor of Science degree in Sociology, Counseling and Creative Writing from the University of Minnesota in 1998. She is working on a collection of poems titled *People Who Feel* and plans to continue publishing in the future.

### Mi Ok Song Bruining

In the time since writing my essay ("A few words...") included in this anthology, I returned to Korea in Oct. '96, to learn Korean, search for my birth mother, teach English for income, work on my book & travel around Korea. At this writing (June '97), my birth mother found me in Jan. '97, & a few days later, I returned to Cambridge, MA for one month to prepare for a longer stay in Korea.

I currently live in Seoul, teach English at Hong-Ik University & am slowly working on my book. Learning Korean is slow & frustrating, yet there is some progress with the help of many Korean friends. Despite occasional severe bouts of homesickness for my cat, Fiona Feline, my '78 VW bus, "Lulu", my friends & family, I have discovered the joys & madness of Seoul, the ironies of Korean culture, met many other feminists here, & am reconnecting with my birth mother.

Finally, there is a collective voice for those of us who have been silent or silenced in the adoption triad & in society.

### K. Burdette

K. Burdette is an American-born adoptee of Korean and German-Irish descent. She received her B.A. in Radio, Television and Film from the University of Maryland at College Park. Her writing has been published in *Link: A Critical Journal on the Arts in Baltimore and the World*, the anthology *Generation Q*, and numerous Washington, D.C. area periodicals. Her recent video work has screened at regional and international festivals across the country. Recently, she has worked as a photojournalist, teacher of film theory, and internet guru. She is currently finishing her master's degree.

### Crystal Lee Hyun Joo Chappell

Born Lee Hyun Joo, I lived in Kwangju with my birthparents, sister and younger brother. We three children were adopted by the same family in 1978 and joined our older brother, who is also a Korean adoptee but not our blood relative.

I became Crystal Chappell. I grew up in a terribly quaint, predominantly white small town near Lansing, MI. For most of my life, I ignored my race and thought I was white. Years later at Northwestern University, I had an "awakening" and joined the struggle to create an Asian American Studies program. Later that year, I found my birthmother. This past summer, my sister, younger brother and I returned to Korea for the first time to meet our birthmother. For the time being, I am both Crystal and Hyun Joo. Currently, I work as a journalist for the Philadelphia Inquirer.

### Eun Jung Che

Eun Jung Che was raised in the northern suburbs of Minneapolis. She was a member of the Adopted Korean Women's group, with whom she had the privilege of performing. She graduated from the University of Minnesota with a degree in Multicultural Studies. Currently, she is a graduate student at George Washington University in Washington, D.C., studying American Civilization and has just completed her first novel, *Keeping Company With Ghosts (You Are Mine)* (working title).

### Thomas Park Clement

Thomas Clement was born in Korea in 1950 or 1951 and was adopted at age 6 or 7. He grew up in Massachusetts, and earned a degree in Psychology from Indiana University and two degrees in Electrical Engineering from Purdue University.

Currently he is the President, CEO, and owner of Mectra Laboratories, Inc. which manufactures and distributes proprietary laparoscopic surgical instruments worldwide. He holds two dozen U.S. medical device patents with 5 more pending.

He is currently a board member of AKA-US (Association of Korean Adoptees, United States).

### Sherilyn Cockroft

Sherlilyn Cockroft was adopted at the age of $9^{1/2}$ on January 29, 1976. Living in the Midwest, she attended Evangel College, a small liberal arts college, where she obtained her Bachelor's degree in Business Administration. After college, she moved to Kansas City, Missouri and worked at the University of Missouri at Kansas City Teaching Hospital, Truman Medical Center. About a year later, she moved to Huntington Beach, California and got involved in the construction industry. Her primary employment has been as an outside sales representative for manufacturing companies who provide supplies for the construction industry.

Currently, she is 30 years old and lives in Long Beach, California. She is aspiring to obtain her Master's degree in business as well as go to Korea to teach English, learn Korean, and find her biological family.

### William Drucker

William Drucker, formerly Ro In Kuk, is Bill to his friends. He lives and works in Vienna, Virginia. He has lived in New York City, Ohio, Connecticut, and Florida. Despite the different locations, he has spent most of the time working as a technical writer. In his 43 years, he is most proud of his two daughters, Lauren and Lindsay. He is divorced.

He considers himself an American. He has little interest in seeing the country of his birth and he does not speak Korean much anymore.

### Zoli Seuk Kim Hall

Zoli Seuk Kim Hall is a writer and artist living in Minneapolis. Her writings have most recently been published in *Colours*, The Asian American Renaissance Journal's *Sticky Rice: The Power of Community* and *Moonrabbit Review*. She will have poems forthcoming in the anthology *Raw Like Sushi*.

### Melissa Lin Hanson

I was born Chang Myoung Hee in Pusan, South Korea in 1970. I am the third of four children born to my parents and the only child to have been adopted. In 1972, I came to the United States to become the oldest child in my adoptive family. The poem that appears in this anthology was written when I had just located my birth family after having grown up with no knowledge of them. Though those were lonely years, as my *unni* (older sister) says, our years to come together are going to be far more than the years we spent apart.

### Lee Herrick

Lee Herrick was born in Seoul in 1970 and adopted at 11 months. He was raised in California and received his MA in Composition and Rhetoric from California State University, Stanislaus. His poetry has appeared in *The New Voice*, *The Poets' Edge*, *South Ash Press*, and *The Korea Times*, among others, and is forthcoming in *dIS*orient* and *Penumbra*. He is the founding editor of the California-based literary magazine, *In the Grove* and teaches writing full-time at Fresno City College.

### Amy Kashiwabara

I was born in Seoul, Korea in 1973. After the death of my natural father, I was brought to the United States by a nun and adopted by my natural grand-aunt and her Japanese-American husband.

So, I am Korean-American with a Japanese name. I am an adopted child who shares a bloodline with her adopted mother. I know nothing about my natural mother.

I love poetry and American politics. I have taught poetry through California Poets in the Schools and worked for the California Democratic Party during the 1996 election. Jackie Kay, Thom Gunn, Lyn Heijinian, and Peter Dale Scott have been a few of my most influential poetry teachers.

My educaton includes a B.A. from U.C. Berkeley in Political Science and ongoing studies at Stanford Law School.

### *Ellwyn Kauffman*

My adoption story is not an anecdote that simply adds another layer of complexity to my life. The fact that I am Korean adopted is not incidental. Rather, it is something of a starting point for getting to the essence of who I am. It is vital to my self understanding. For the longest time I was reluctant to write about my experiences growing up as a Korean adoptee. I promised myself I would write about it one day, but given the emotionally charged nature of the topic, I had doubts about being able to handle it objectively and truthfully. I used to think what I would need to write about my adoption experience was distance, a span of time between me and my past large enough to think back over the years with a cool, even-tempered sensibility. But recently I've come to realize my past will never be this far away. And more than objectivity or perspective, a sharper self-awareness is what brings my story alive. For me, that critical level of self-awareness has only come about because of recent experiences with other Korean adoptees.

"Bulgogi" is taken from journal entries, and pieced together with an account of my disastrous first attempt at Korean cooking. "Never" was hammered out late one night in frustration over the preconceptions and expectations that Korean adoptees are sometimes, and unfairly held to.

### *Mihee-Nathalie Lemoine (a.k.a. Cho Mihee, Kim Byul)*

Mihee-Nathalie Lemoine uses her Korean birthname "Kim (Gold) Byul (Star)" when she writes. Born in Pusan in 1968, she was adopted in 1969 by a Belgian family. After her second trip to Korea in 1991, she found her "Korean" mother. In December of 1991, she co-founded the Euro-Korean League, the first national

Korean adoptees group in Belgium.

In 1994, she co-founded the first Korean adoptee group in Korea to help them in their search. She assisted over 80 Korean adoptees search/find/reunite (with) their birth-families.

Currently she lives (since 1993) in Seoul, Korea and works as an artist/painter/filmmaker/writer and activist. She's also an initiator/co-founder/member of KameleonZ (Korean Overseas Multimedia Artists group) and she is a co-founder/coordinator of Han Diaspora, a yearly multimedia art performance on Diaspora/displacement.

### Beth Kyong Lo

Beth Kyong Lo was found as a newborn in Seoul, Korea in 1975 and came to Minneapolis five months later through Children's Home Society. She is married to a Hmong American and has two kids.

She has been writing since she was in the fourth grade and always knew she wanted to be a writer. In her writing she explores her own identity as an Asian American, an adoptee raised in an urban setting, a mother, a "Hmong" wife, and birth mother images, all in forms of prose and poetry. She was just announced as a finalist of a contest put on by *The Loft and Colors Magazine: Journey From Anger to Wisdom* with an essay, "Laughter in Iowa," expressing her frustration at the racism that occurs in her Caucasian family. She has also participated in mentoring Asian American students through the Asian American Renaissance, has worked with New York-based performing poets, Cayenne, and has had an essay on her experience with Asian gangs published back in 1992 in *Colors Magazine, "It's Just A Street Thing"*.

Currently, she is working on a novel about a Korean adopted woman and her bi-cultural daughters--how hard it is for all of them dealing with the definitions of being "real" Asian and how it has affected their family. Beth is completing her B.A. in English at Augsburg College and hopes to start an MFA program in the Fall of 1998.

### Kim Maher

I arrived at LAX on November 1, 1956 from Korea at 21 months of age to an Air Force sergeant and his wife who anxiously awaited their first child. They had tried for many years to adopt domestically but nothing had ever worked out. Upon hearing that a couple from Oregon, Harry and Bertha Holt, had adopted eight children from Korea and were helping other people in this endeavor, my future mother and father decided that this chance to have their own child was a blessing from God. They perservered and eight months later, they had their new, malnourished, scared baby girl. I flew over to America sitting on the lap of Grandma Bertha Holt so an extra seat would not have to be taken on the plane.

Prejudice ran rampant in those early days of transracial families but my parents were made of the stuff to break new ground. My sister, Robin, was added to the family 2 years later and we grew up in a middle class neighborhood in a suburb of Los Angeles. Our family was normal in most ways except always being aware that our Korean looks made us stand out among our Caucasian friends.

Now, I am married with a total of three children, two of whom are daughters who are adopted domestically. One is of European ancestry and one is of Vietnamese. Again, my life and family reflect the ongoing love and challenge of "Being Adopted".

### David Miller

David Miller lives in Fairfield, California and is studying business management. He hopes to work in international business. One of his goals is to one day finally go to Korea, not necessarily to search for anyone, but just to see what it's like. He believes that it is necessary for adoptees to have more of a voice.

"I believe every adoptee should consider themselves special--part of a special family. To people having a problem with adoption, feeling like they have to choose between identities, they should know that eventually, the turmoil will die down and that they are very lucky to experience two worlds. Take the best from both of them and use the best things to help other people. I was fortunate to grow up in a diverse area, but to those people living in more remote areas, I encourage them to see as much of the world as possible so they will know there's more than what they are exposed to. They will find that they are not alone."

## Nabiya

I was born in Pusan, spent three years at the Namkwang Children's Home and then was adopted through Korean Social Services. My Korean name is Mi Hyun (Chung), but was given to me by the orphanage, not my parents, so I only go by Mi Hyun when addressed in Korean. I am conducting a search for a mother who doesn't want to be found and a father who doesn't know I exist (more than likely, given the circumstances of my death).

In the meantime, I am a junior at Westmar University in LeMars, Iowa. I am double majoring in East Asian Studies and International Relations, having spent the last year as an exchange student at Ewha Women's University in Seoul, Korea. I grew up in Park Rapids, Minnesota, a small town in the northern part of the state.

I have been writing since I was in grade school. It was a way for me to talk to someone who understood me without having to try to explain myself (me). I have not taken any formal writing classes, but have had several poems published through various anthologies, along with the publication of contest-winning essays. Several of my poems were published under the pen name: *Nabiya*. In Korean, *na-bi-ya* would mean something along the lines of "the butterfly". I chose this as my pen name, idolizing the life of the butterfly, the freedom and delicate beauty, and personalizing it by making it Korean. This is what I strive for in my writing and in my life.

## Su Niles

Su Niles was born in Seoul, Korea in 1959 and was among the first of the Korean-born adoptees to come to America. Raised in Sacramento, California, she lives there still, and has become involved in the Korean American community. In May 1994, Su began an Adult Adoptee group now called Hanmi Yang-Ja Yang-yeo Whae. Additionally, she serves as a board member on Friends of Korea, an international non-profit organization, and as a board member on the Sacramento Chapter of the Korean American Coalition. Su has had poems and essays published in *Roots & Wings*, a publication for families of Intercountry Adoption; *We (Woori)* magazine; and *KoreAm Journal*.

### Sam Rogers (Kim Sun Il)

Sam Rogers was born in Inch'on, South Korea. He is now eighteen years old and lives with an American father, Australian mother and two biological sisters. His favorite hobbies are collecting CDs, playing football and baseball.

### Kari Ruth

Kari Ruth serves on the board of MAK (Minnesota Adopted Koreans), an organization for adult adopted Koreans. She was adopted when she was approximately 6 months old from Seoul, Korea, and has lived in Minnesota since that time.

Kari does not believe in a "middle ground" for adoptees who are formulating their racial identities. She does not choose to straddle a multicultural fence. She believes in forging new ground; a space of her own. A space where racial identity is neither bound by traditional nor mainstream definitions of race and culture. A space where she is free to be a person rather than live by the confines of a label.

### Leah Sieck

Seoul: three months old, and I leave for the States. Twenty-three years in the States, living with my adoptive family: European-American parents Bob and Holly Sieck and my adopted Vietnamese-Cambodian-American brother Fredo Sieck.

My parents always said I could return to Korea and search for my birthparents. So I did in 1996. In Korea, I have been welcomed by many Koreans, but the deepest bond and constant dialogue have been with Hio Kyeng Lee, my Korean-American roommate, friend, and intellectual and spiritual partner. Coming to Korea has been a journey through sorrow (*han*) and ecstasy (*heung*). Sorrow because the difficulty relearning my mother tongue and Korean ways recalls my 23 years in the States of searching and hungering for my Korean roots. Ecstasy because the life force of the Korean people resounds in the drumming of *poongmul* (farmer's drumming) and soars in their shamanic spirit.

For me, the soul of Korea is woman. As I explore and proclaim my difference as an adopted, Korean-American, middle class, shamanic woman, I share the fears and the joys of embodying difference. I am searching for my birthparents and I am loving my adoptive parents. I am trying to honor myself, my two cultures and my international family. I am determined not to split apart. Someday, *Omoni*, I will meet you, or perhaps you are always with me. I respect your decision. It is not easy to be a woman in Korea.

### Kari Smalkoski
Kari Smalkoski was found in Seoul and adopted through Holt and Children's Home Society of Minnesota at the age of six months. She was raised in a suburb of Minneapolis, Minnesota and presently resides in Minneapolis. In 1996, she received a literary grant from the national organization, Money for Women, for her book in progress, *Notes on Hunger*. Excerpts will be published in the Spring 1997 issue of *Moonrabbit Review* and the Fall/Winter 1997 issue of *The Asian Pacific American Journal*.

Kari Smalkoski is a faculty member at the College of Saint Catherine.

### Rebecca Smith
Rebecca Smith is 28 years old and was adopted at the age of 18 months. She grew up mainly in Northern Illinois, though she has also lived in South Carolina for a few years. She now resides in San Diego where she has lived for the past 10 years. She has an older brother who is not adopted and her parents are divorced. She has a Bachelor's degree in psychology, although she's returning to school to study graphic design. Her interests are drawing and writing.

### Rebekah Jin Turner
Rebekah Jin Turner (Kim, Jin Ee) is 23 years old and was adopted from Seoul, Korea at the age of seven months through Holt International Children's Services. She was raised in Michigan and attended Michigan State University, majoring in Family Community Services. She has just recently moved to Los Angeles, California and is a first-year graduate student at UCLA (Masters of Social Welfare program) where she serves as the co-chair of the API caucus for Social Welfare students. She has had the opportunity to travel extensively throughout Korea and the Pacific Rim.

"The poem I wrote for the anthology describes, in my personal opinion, the chaos and confusion many adoptees may feel if they have had the experience of growing up in a dysfunctional home. Often times, many of the difficult family situations we find ourselves in have nothing to do with the fact that we are adopted."

## *YoungHee*
YoungHee is a twenty-eight year old Korean adoptee and has attended various colleges on and off for a total of five years. She dropped out many times to travel, rock climb, and make money. The longest she has lived in one place in the last four years is eight months. Mostly she is homeless by choice, living in different national parks, fastidiously avoiding rangers, and enjoying a rock climber's lifestyle. Her essay explores her own internalized oppression.

# Editors' Notes

***Tonya Bishoff*** was born in Korea and adopted by Caucasian parents at the age of 16 months. She has earned a B.A. (English) from U.C. Berkeley and M.A. (English) from Chapman University. Her writings have appeared in various publications including *dIS\*ori - ent Journalzine, writing away here: a korean-american anthology, WE (Woori) Magazine* and the forthcoming *Scaling the Chord.*

***Jo Rankin*** (Jung Im Hong) was born in Inchon, Korea in 1967, adopted by American parents in 1969, and raised in San Diego. She earned her degree in Journalism, then worked for two PBS stations for eight years. She co-founded the Association of Korean Adoptees (AKA) in 1994. She has appeared in *A Magazine, Asian Pages, dIS\*orient Journalzine, Glendale News Press, KoreAm Journal, Korea Central Daily, Korea Times, Korean Quarterly, Southern California Business Journal,* and *WE (Woori) Magazine.*

# Afterword

This journey toward publication began in the summer of 1996. As adoptees, we are both very close to the issues at hand. For this reason, we have been extremely protective of its integrity from conception to birth. We initially requested submissions by/about Korean adoptees, searching for work which might offer glimpses into the complexities of transracial adoption. A wide variety of sources responded, including parents and associates of adoptees.

Faced with the startling fact that many adoptees were writing for themselves, we decided to narrow the focus of the anthology to works written exclusively by Korean adoptees. This forced us to confront issues of inclusivity/exclusivity--issues adoptees face daily. In choosing this route, we hope to offer a collection that may inspire in its specificity. By no means do we see it as definitive of the Korean adoptee community. We do, however, envision it as a starting point, the first stage of many more projects to come.